The
Amaryllis
Picotee

The Amaryllis Picotee

RICHARD SMITH

PALMETTO

P U B L I S H I N G

Charleston, SC

www.PalmettoPublishing.com

Hardcover ISBN: 979-8-8229-5338-3
Paperback ISBN: 979-8-8229-5339-0

Table of Contents

Johnnie

Ivannes
Killer Wasps
Mr. Alfred Hitchcock
Afternoon Naps
Pop Goes the Weasel

His name was Johnnie. How or why the "ie" got tagged on to the end instead of the "y" or just nothing at all is anybody's guess. Maybe it was an accident. Maybe it was not. In some cases, names have meaning as to the essence of the person so labeled. Often, names get passed on because they're popular or some favorite relative or movie star or politician or ex-secret sweetheart possessed said nomenclature. Maybe the name follows the right DNA track concerning the character of the person involved. Maybe it doesn't. It is worth the time for people to look up the meaning of names, ferreting out any paradoxes, contrasts to reality, or singular jokes regarding the newly arrived. Anger, frustration, and tears might be alleviated—maybe.

"John," according to Mr. Webster, means "the Lord is gracious." That was certainly true in this case. Its roots come from the Hebrew word *yehonathan* and the Greek word *Ivannes*. But back to this "ie" instead of "y" business. To me, adding a "y" to a name indicates a closer chip off the old block, a closer extension of the main gene pool—a little acorn spermatozoon under the mighty oak of the forest. "Ie" does the same thing but carries it one step further by adding a certain flavor.

1

It sensitizes it. It turns hardwood into softwood. A certain light casts itself as little oak turns into weeping willow or pink dogwood.

The offshoot from the type "A" becomes small "a" and starts hanging around other vowels. It nurtures life by giving it sounds and expressions that add depth and meaning to humanity that would not be there otherwise. Small a's often become shepherds and shepherdesses among Arcadian hills, rather than rough, hewing trailblazers through Rocky Mountains. And in this case, the "ie" for this *yehonathan*, this *Ivannes*, had the same effect on the protagonist of this long, short story, little seven-year-old Johnnie. When it all comes down to it, the decision of adding the "ie," however thought out or flippant, was prophetic. There was some unconscious intent. There was some subterranean motivation of Greek mythic proportions of parental or outside forces. For him, truth was reflected in the essence of the name Johnnie no matter how you try to change or dress it up. He made choices made within the framework of what was going to be. Ergo, Aeneas had better get himself to Latium, or else there was going to be hell to pay. Maybe that is how the "ie" got there.

It was also prophetic in the sense that something predicted is often singular until looking back at it. When you first heard it, somehow you questioned its veracity. You did not have the eyes to see, nor the ears to hear, because when you originally were seeing and hearing, the glass was dim and dark. Fortunately, his guardian angels protected the rough-hewed splinters in Johnnie's destiny from interference.

Johnnie's mother was in labor after the water broke for well over twenty-four hours. He wasn't interested as to what the world had to offer—at first. But once he arrived, the discovery of story intrigued him. It beckoned. It was what he first remembered. Not the ones that adults read to children—although there were some fairy tales he was exposed to like the "who's the fairest among them all" wicked stepmother queen—but stories he made up. His first saga was in the front yard around the cedar bush next to the front porch of his home. It was there—at that cedar bush—that Johnnie "wrote" his first story. It was all in his spirit and body. He was so engrossed, so enamored, so enabled that time and space melted into the background as the saga came together and took shape. Hallowed high noon was bringing a joyous surprise. Alas, eyes were forgetting themselves in the creation, alas, 'twas in that experience to know *vocare*—a vocation.

The tale contained discovery, danger, and delights. Out and in, through and among, did Johnnie's spaceship—a popsicle stick—fly betwixt and between the branches of the cedar bush looking for safety, the "top secret," or the end of the rainbow that would save the world from mass destruction.

Watch out! Killer wasps! Aliens from another world appeared ready to sting, to bring the explorers in their spaceship to an end. Down into the heart of the matter and into the bush traveled the faithful warriors.

Oh no! One of our men has been captured, and although it was only one out of the mighty hundred, that did not matter because the brave, dedicated warriors knew that when one was in danger, they all were in danger.

The attack begins! The rescuer hammers away with his weaponry. In and out and up and down among the cedar branches he flew with a slither of thin, gray smoke drifting from behind his spaceship, signifying the trail traveled. He just misses the venomous stinger. Then suddenly, at the final moment when he almost gives up because of the mortar attacks from the enemy and exhaustion from within, he saves the lost one. They whisk away, darting and daring to and fro through the cedar branches at high speed, flying into home at the top of the cedar bush in the twinkling of an eye.

Safe at last!

The End.

He had seen that on television a lot. He liked the way it put a period at the end of the story. It told you it was time to move on to other things. Sometimes that was good. Sometimes it was not.

There was not much to recall during his early encounter with television, with the exception of Tuesday nights. It became a source of trial and temptation. After having said his prayers one full moon-lit evening, thanking God for everybody and everything, including the stars in heaven and Cyndy, his pet Chihuahua (Notice her name ended in a "y.") Johnnie did not like her. She was always hiding underneath the couch, growling and spitting, whenever he tried to play with her.), and after the last of several "amens," his mother left his bedroom.

Johnnie counted to a hundred. His mother taught him this exercise. It added to his sense of justification for what followed. He sneaked back into the hallway next to the den where the television lived. His goal was to watch Mr. Hitchcock of *Alfred Hitchcock Presents*, with his mother none the wiser. His mother told him he would not understand those stories, and also, it came on way past his bedtime. But Johnnie liked Mr. Hitchcock. He had never heard anybody sound like that in his immediate world. Mr. Hitchcock sounded smart and all-knowing and looked like a favorite uncle of his who was always giving him flavored chewing gum. He certainly would have liked Mr. Hitchcock to read him fairy tales rather than his mother.

After maneuvering himself in the hallway to the right of the entrance to the den, he had a direct sight line to the television screen, and at the same time, he was able to keep an eye on the back of the couch where his mother sat scratching the back of Johnnie's father's head. They were watching Mr. Hitchcock, with Johnnie watching all three of them from the rear. His mother's head seldom moved. Thank goodness it did not and thank goodness that her eyes were only in front of her head during those perilous times. After Mr. Hitchcock left and the sponsor's commercial was shown, Johnnie bowed his head, thanking God for Mr. Hitchcock as well. He then quietly slipped back to his bedroom for the evening.

It was later in the same era of his life that he thought up another story. But this time he put feet and distance to it. His own it was. It issued from out of his head. He kneaded it into the reality of things. This time it brought discovery, exposing hidden dangers in exploration.

One of the "thou shalts" in Johnnie's early life was the dreaded afternoon nap. As an adult, he came to appreciate such things, but to a small child, afternoon naps were like eating liver and spinach in the same meal. However, he did try to like the latter later. He would watch *Popeye the Sailor Man* on occasion. When Popeye ate his spinach— BINGO—he was strong and suddenly possessed big arm muscles. Johnnie desired the same. It was a classic example of lusting. Although at the time he did not know to call it that. He asked his mother to buy spinach at the grocery store.

She smiled a knowing smile and asked, "Are you sure?"

"Yes, mother," responded Johnnie, although with less assurance.

Later that evening at supper, he made the attempt to satisfy his lust for big arm muscles with no sweat. He nearly threw up. This was most disconcerting. It made reality hard to swallow. He was going to have to get big arm muscles some other way. It was a most difficult trial. The whole experience and the spinach left a bad taste in his mouth.

But back to afternoon naps. Mother also took a nap with him. She was a true believer in micromanagement. She also believed in the use of thin, scraggy branches from hickory trees that stung when applied to the buttocks and legs of disobedient little boys. She gave little credence to the "inner, innocent child in all of us" theory and adhered more to the rudimentary tenets of Hyper-Calvinism and the doctrine of original sin.

On this particular afternoon, Johnnie's mother was in one of Mr. Dante's Empyrean circles of the Paradiso, deep in sleep and dead to the world and with a slight smile on her face. She was so deep in sleep that she knew nothing of the unfolding reality of the moment when Johnnie slowly eased out of her arms, all the while listening to her slight snore that had kind of a musical rhythm to it. He knew that any break in tempo might mean she was about to wake up. But the snore held steady, so he gently slid out of the folds of a loving embrace. He quietly tiptoed away until he was out of the house and out of hearing range and into his own personal Paradiso—his backyard with the old rusty swing set. With arms outstretched, he flew over to a weeping willow tree he had recently planted, flying as if he was in his own stick spaceship.

Suddenly, off in the distance, something glistened in the sunlight. It intrigued him. It beckoned. It became the apple of his eye. It was a new swing set with a shiny swinging rocket beyond the fence in his neighbor's backyard. It kind of looked like the spaceships he imagined at the cedar bush. A choice presented itself. He listened for his mother's voice but heard only silence. He decided to take just a little nibble and chew and then back to home port. So over the fence he went.

Ah, the thrill of his new rocket ride, back and forth, flying through the air with the greatest of ease, having his cake and eating it, too, with an eye cast toward home in case his mother woke up from her journey, calling for him from the back porch. From this view he saw the world from a different angle of repose, when suddenly off in the distance his eye caught sight of another apple he never could have seen from his own backyard. It was a tall, shiny sliding board in the backyard of his neighbor's neighbor, away from Johnnie's house.

"If only I could slide once. Only once," Johnnie thought.

So to the sliding board of the neighbor's neighbor, he went. He couldn't see his home anymore, but he convinced himself that he could still hear his mother's voice. After deftly crawling over a picket fence with stiletto points and meandering budding roses of Sharon, with one eye on killer wasps, he made his way toward the shiny, silver board, glistening in the sunlight. And this time his encounter with said board was more than a nibble and chew; it was a downright chomping down of a feast. He ate and ate of the experience. One slide turned into a many splendored things until a sweat broke out on his brow. After a while, though, he became winded. He decided to rest from discovery. But discovery is a fickle creature. It decided to announce itself without an invitation from him. His eye caught something unusual occurring in the front yard of his neighbor's neighbor.

It was a little bird, chirping and hopping around.

But it was not flying like other little birds and travelers in spaceships. It would stop. Look around. Then it would chirp in a high-pitched voice and start hopping around again like a small rabbit. Now this was strange for two reasons. First, this was no rabbit. And second, the chirping was not like what you normally hear from a nest of hungry baby birds, or when they were acknowledging the rising of the sun in the morning. None of the notes from this little bird camped out on pretty tunes, but rather on sorrowful, pleading ones that went from one short shrill to the next. Johnnie felt his heart tugged, singing in response to the pleas like an opera diva. So he decided to check matters out.

As he tiptoed to the front yard, so as not to frighten the little, chirpy bird, he noticed out of the periphery of his right eye another creature tiptoeing from the periphery of the front yard. Only this creature's tiptoeing possessed a sinister elegance and grace with its head abnormally, threateningly extended forward, with an equally abnormally, threateningly extended body, with an accompanying tail that meandered back and forth very slowly. Johnnie froze. He wasn't too keen on the appearance of this creature, especially its tail.

Johnnie didn't like tails for some reason. He was glad he didn't have one. Although a babysitter once told him he acted like he did. She also said other things that weren't polite after Johnnie told his mother that the babysitter had been smoking cigarettes in the backyard while his mother was away. You see, the babysitter promised Johnnie a nickel and a piece of candy if he wouldn't say anything about her smoking to his mother. But the nickel and piece of candy never went beyond sweet nothings and sugar plums dancing in his head. Johnnie felt at that point no obligation to keep his part of the agreement, since the first party had not fulfilled its obligations on her side of said agreement. So, while his mother was driving the babysitter home, Johnnie proceeded to spill the beans to his mother, including short coughs now and then in his telling for dramatic effect.

The babysitter from that point on was history. Johnnie doesn't remember what was exactly said as they rounded the last corner to the babysitter's house, but he does remember it was short and not sweet. He also remembered the babysitter slamming the car door upon arrival, while using the word "brat" and other short words he didn't know the meaning of, with his mother driving back home in record time. The whole incident made Johnnie very happy. He felt a tinge of joy because this babysitter possessed a mean, cynical disposition, although at the time Johnnie didn't know to call it that. He only knew she talked sassily, always had a frown on her face, and most of all wasn't pretty like Johnnie's favorite babysitter, Sally. She always took him to go see cartoon films.

But back to the tiptoeing creature with the meandering tail who was eyeing the little, chirpy bird.

Of course, this other creature was a big, fat tomcat with many lives. He had a checkered past and was the father of countless kittens in the neighborhood. This big, fat tomcat was eyeing the little, chirpy bird while Johnnie was eyeing them both. Johnnie knew he had to rescue Little Chirpy. He imagined himself like the head space warrior in the cedar bush and immediately started yelling and screaming running at both creatures.

"Scat! Scat! Scat!" Johnnie cried while doing a two-step dance move.

The tomcat's response was a hiss, and he didn't move. He started eyeing Johnnie.

"Scat! Scat! Scat!" Johnnie cried as he repeated his two-step.

The big, fat tomcat repeated his hiss and added a perturbed, deep-throated meow. He then gave Johnnie a snooty, snotty, scum-of-the-earth look and walked away.

By this time, Little Chirpy was going wild, screeching and hopping all over the place like a chicken with its head cut off. Johnnie thought about what to do for about two seconds. He tiptoed over to Little Chirpy, scooping the little bird in his hands. Immediately, it ceased its shrieks and began stretching its long, thin neck into the air like the giraffes reaching for the leaves to eat from tree branches Johnnie had seen in nature magazines.

In the calm of the moment, after Little Chirpy settled down, Johnnie heard other high-pitched voices in the air. He looked around to see where the sounds came from. The sun glistened as the wind blew. In the twinkling of an eye, he looked toward the heavens. Off in the near distance of about three feet, he saw a tiny stick and pine straw nest cradled at the juncture of three small branches of a blooming, pink dogwood tree.

"That must be your home," whispered Johnnie. "And those must be your little brothers and sisters I hear. And you tried to fly, I bet, but couldn't just yet."

Johnnie knew what his next step should be. He walked toward Little Chirpy's home port. He slowly and carefully climbed onto one of the lower limbs of the pink dogwood tree while holding Little Chirpy close to his heart.

"If I hurt you, I'm sorry. This is new to me, too," said Johnnie.

He then carefully placed Little Chirpy in the tiny nest. His brothers and sisters were quiet. He thought about Little Chirpy's mother. He decided it was probably a good time to leave before she came home from shopping. He didn't want Mother Chirpy to think he was up to no good. He then thought of his own mother. He decided it was probably a good time for him to go home, too, or at least get within hearing range of her voice.

But then suddenly something caught his eye across the street from the front yard of his neighbor's neighbor, which was farther away from Johnnie's home. It was the biggest tree Johnnie had ever seen. It was the granddaddy of all trees in the neighborhood. It was the king of the hill on top of the world. The wind began to blow in earnest, majestically flapping its leaves as if calling Johnnie to come explore.

"I bet it would be fun to climb to the top of that tree," thought Johnnie. "I bet I could see all the way home and back. I bet even to China and back. I'll just climb up a branch or two and see if mother is looking for me. Then I will go right home."

So off he went, oblivious to anything but the journey. He scooted up the steep hill. He hugged the tree upon arrival, and then scampered up the lowest limb with the aid of knotholes in the tree's trunk. Then he climbed to the next limb, which was very close above. And then to the next and then to the next. Johnnie paused to catch his breath and his heart. He looked around the mighty hardwood with long, meandering limbs and leaves as big as his hand, twisting and turning in random fashion skyward. He looked out to see frontiers and paths never seen before. He looked toward his home. He could see only dimly the trails he took to this spot, revealing something familiar, yet slightly askew, seen from this height.

This view offered a fresh insight of the familiar in the context of a wider world. He looked for Little Chirpy's home but saw only clumps of gathered leaves. He thought of what he had seen, where he had been, knowing he never could capture fully the truth of the matter. All this he felt, but he did not know the words to articulate the effect until many years later when looking back at this traveled trail. He felt the joy of surprise with great intensity—an arrow of love, not expected or sought but shot from out of the blue, where rainbows gather among stormy clouds. The arrow had a flaming intensity that pierced into his heart, soul, and mind.

Off to the east, the wind blew more strongly. It directed his head away from home to the rational, tall, vertical, literalist loblolly pines in sandy soil. The east wind further directed his eyes and ears down the street away from his home to a slightly familiar figure running toward him beyond a chain-link fence enclosing a square, treeless backyard. A branch hit him on the head from the hand of the majestic hardwood, let loose by the east wind.

"Johnnie!" yelled the running, familiar figure.

"Johnnie!" yelled again the close friend of Johnnie's mother.

"Johnnie!" yelled once again he knew by instinct was trouble with a capital "T."

A sinking feeling arose as he climbed down the majestic hardwood, descending into the valley of sane pines, and slowly walking toward the chain-link fence that separated him and the quickly evaporating paradise from his immediate, stormy future coming at him in overdrive.

"Where the h--- have you been?!" blasted the very close friend of Johnnie's mother.

Johnnie knew he had not been there but also knew by instinct he was about to enter into its domain. He also knew it was best not to argue the point.

"Your mother is worried to death and crying her eyes out! The sheriff is out looking for you! Your father is on the way home from work! Where in the h--- have you been?!"

Johnnie was scared to death. He stood there working up a sweat thinking about the "h" word again. He thought about the times the preacher used that word on Sunday mornings during his sermon in conjunction with pain and suffering and the weeping and gnashing of teeth.

"Come here!"

Johnnie hesitated and pondered the wisdom of doing such a thing.

"Get your b--- over the fence this instant!"

Now that was a word he never heard the preacher use on Sunday mornings. By instinct, he knew his mother's close friend was about to cross some sort of thin red line. So over the fence he went. Goodbye, heaven! Hello, brave new world!

"Do you realize what you have done?!"

It was unfortunately beginning to dawn on him.

"I'm taking you home after I call your mother, if she's still alive! Get in my car and don't even think about leaving or there will be h--- to pay!"

"What do you mean by 'will be'?" Johnnie thought.

He obeyed, but very reluctantly. The refining fire was limiting free expression. And what happened in the next twenty minutes of Johnnie's life was a whirlwind of words and more words filled with anger and tears. Courage and fear raised their heads in new forms. Spirit and flesh converged to do battle. And in its heat, his b--- received further attention from the backhand of his father, while the sounds of his mother's weeping filled the room.

And before he knew it, Johnnie was back in his bedroom where this saga began, crying and rubbing the sting out of his buttocks. He felt his head throbbing where the branch had struck uninvited. He began another wave of tears. He felt downright defeated and not at all cheerful.

He heard his father's car backing out of the driveway to go back to work. He pulled his toys and wooden blocks out of the closet to build a new city and create a new story. He thought about what he said to his newfound friend, his very own "Jonathan"—Little Chirpy.

"You tried to fly, I bet, but couldn't just yet."

He then thought of the majestic hardwood and the feeling he felt out of the blue in its arms. Revisiting those paths took a little bit of the sting out of the situation. By instinct, he knew there were things done and things left undone that called for a confession. But also by instinct, he knew that in some mysterious, crazy, thorn-in-the-flesh way, the power and the glory of it all seeped through.

He looked at his jack-in-the-box. Turn the handle around long enough, listen to the tune, and just at the right moment, "Pop Goes the Weasel." He did just that and "pop" went the weasel. He smiled. He continued building his new city and new story, making a vow to be, if not always faithful to the idea of afternoon naps, at least faithful to its observance.

The Mighty Oak Tree

Clash of the Gene Pools
Hearing Santa Claus
Ruaching Sinterklaas

He fathered Johnnie. This would prove to be the supreme adventure for both of them.

Out of the dust and ashes on a cold, late afternoon in autumn, when Johnnie's father came home early looking for comfort and Johnnie's mother was not into afternoon naps at the time, they begot little Johnnie into time and space. They fashioned a new life, the flesh of their flesh and bones of their bones, in the midst of great excitement and fanfare. And while the flesh was willing, the spirit of the father was weak. It seemed that very little, if any, of the genes from the male gene pool swam its way into Johnnie's being. Familial rumor has it that there must have been some sort of blockage in the canal, or someone was asleep on the job when the transaction took place for the spirit of Johnnie's father to come up so short in Johnnie. The hardwood went soft.

Maybe with the idea of great laughter and foolishness, winking all the way, the One in charge of such matters decided to release something pent up that had been kept at bay in the previous generation, choosing to dress this new being into some sort of blessing in disguise, reminding humanity of the unexpected and unintended placed into the affairs of men and women. And a particular destiny required a shaping of character that, in turn, required a guardian angel making sure the paternal genes stayed unexpressed.

At the beginning, Johnnie felt different from his father. Later, much later, in life, when his affections for Popeye blossomed into affections for Ennis Del Mar, perhaps, just perhaps, Johnnie began to think he was a lot more like his father than he could comprehend. Johnnie's father was an Air Force fighter pilot. Johnnie was captivated by rockets and spaceships. Probably, the truth of the matter was half-hidden in the dappled shadows of overhanging limbs of the mighty oak trees and the weeping willow trees on the same parcel of ground.

The gene pool of Johnnie's mother gained the upper hand in the spirit as well as the flesh in the encounter. There was some sort of passive aggressive play that included a curveball and the stealing of several bases, which resulted in a thrilling slide into home on her team. Or it might have been a come-on, teary-eyed expression that resulted in a karate, Machiavellian maneuver, and machination that used the opponent's own force to turn the tables on himself to cause a slam dunk for the less forceful party. Who knows for sure?

One of the first Christmas mornings Johnnie remembers vividly was when Santa Claus brought him a choo-choo train with accompanying circular track on a large piece of plywood. He also brought an oversized boy doll—a ventriloquist's dummy. It was this same Christmas that, during the evening before, he heard Santa Claus brushing up against the Christmas tree in the next room in the dead of night. It was very dark. And Johnnie was afraid to check things out for fear of scaring Santa Claus away before everything had been unpacked.

On Christmas morning, he figured that Santa Claus had to drop his gifts through the large front room window because there was no chimney or fireplace in the house. The Christmas tree was right in front of the window, so no wonder Johnnie heard the sound of him brushing against the tree. He couldn't, however, see how that train fit in Santa's red sack. It must have been tied to his sled. In the week following, whenever his parents' adult friends asked Johnnie about

Christmas and his presents from Santa Claus, Johnnie always told them about hearing Santa Claus brushing up against the tree. Without fail, a roar of laughter always occurred among the listeners after telling the story. It always left Johnnie a bit confused as to what was so funny about an encounter in the middle of the night that to him was mysterious and a bit scary—that is, until the fourth grade, when Johnnie's father shed light on the particular tale. The world became a somewhat cynical place to Johnnie. He was devastated. But back to this memorable Christmas morning.

Johnnie enjoyed the sounds and smoke of the choo-choo train. He envisioned traveling to strange lands and encountering forces beyond his understanding and control. But the train was circular and the props skimpy, so a certain dullness and boredom set in within fifteen minutes. But his encounter with the oversized boy ventriloquist doll was another story. The doll had some plastic flesh and actually had features that resembled Johnnie—dark brown hair and eyes. The doll's dark brown hair was combed and straight like his when his mother dressed him for Sunday school and church. And as mentioned, the doll had some size to it. It was not like the flimsy, toothpick variety of a girl doll with wavy blond hair and a pair of prominent you-know-whats. Johnnie could hold and hug it just like it was another little boy. And on top of all that, its lower mouth moved up and down, controlled by a long string in back. So Johnnie could talk to the doll and the doll could talk back in Johnnie's higher-pitched voice and would never contradict Johnnie but would always agree with what Johnnie said.

And as Johnnie's mother explained to any of her friends who gave a puzzled, singular look and were brazen enough to inquire about having such a companion, this doll was a doll made for boys. The train track with its stark environs received short attention and an early retirement. Its final demise was left to conjecture and imagination. But the fate of that boy doll was to experience life to the fullest. Oh, how Johnnie loved his boy doll that could talk! What was the total amount of hours of attention lavished would be anybody's guess and would be like counting the grains of sand on the seashore.

Then later they began sharing secrets with each other in Johnnie's bedroom. The boy doll was always there to listen. Then as their relationship developed, the boy doll would talk back and offer a different perspective on matters. The opinions were not rude, nor did the doll interrupt or make fun of, nor did the opinions contain the "h" and "b" words, but were confident whispers of concern like those of a close buddy you wanted to hug every time you saw him—a friend who loved you just because of who you were, who was honest enough to tell you when you wore a T-shirt or shoes or clipped-on Sunday morning bow tie that didn't look good on you.

Most of the time Johnnie made sure his bedroom door was closed and locked. He didn't want anyone listening to their intimate conversations, especially his mother. And no matter how much time had passed since their last conversation, they just picked up where they left off in talking as if no time had passed.

The boy doll's big, brown, wide eyes, the windows of its soul, with shades of anticipatory delight, would look Johnnie full in the face, never avoiding Johnnie's look, never trying to mask in order to deceive or mislead, and never accusing. Just a steady, comforting, vulnerable stare. At times, Johnnie felt he was looking into a mirror of sorts, yet his object of love remained distinctive. In many ways he had met someone cut from the same material, yet there were unique patterns to how they talked and talked and talked with and without words.

Conversation with Johnnie's father was a different story. Thinking back as an adult, Johnnie cannot remember much that was said or not said. His father was always on a mission of some kind, flying off somewhere—remote corners of the world. Johnnie's father did provide. Food was on the table. They never went hungry. Even when financial strain raised its ugly head, a way was found to overcome the adverse circumstances. One Christmas, Johnnie and his mother decorated a small, silver artificial tree with miniscule, dark blue ball ornaments.

That year the huge, green fir tree that permeated the house with an aroma that quickened the spirit was a stranger. But there was a comfort in the activity of dressing the silver tree, a closeness with his mother that raised its beautiful, glistening head many years after.

Maybe, just maybe, if Johnnie had been able to go up in one of those jets that took his father away, Johnnie would have understood his world better and discovered people and places that he could bring back to the cedar bush. It seemed the backside of matters kept cropping up instead. The backside of a hand with the backside of Johnnie on occasion. The backside of two heads staring in opposite directions, one going out the front door for the next flight, the other heading for the bedroom for another conversation with the boy doll. Or did memory tell only part of the story, or in some way distort some gesture? Were there caverns unexplored that might have given a fuller explanation? Perhaps it is too easy to say that the animal, vegetable material was all that connected hardwood to softwood.

But after disturbing Mount Vesuvius with the adventurous afternoon in the neighborhood, Pompei treaded lightly. He had experienced the volcanic eruption, however justified. And if rumblings were even remotely heard, a sort of subservience with not entirely honorable motivations set in until the coast was clear. A chill set in. A massive stone moat was built. The drawbridge went down occasionally. A free flow of exchange in word and deed never really took root that held. Although there was the occasional oasis. The very same day that Johnnie's father told him the truth about that jolly man with ruddy cheeks, sled, red sack, and reindeer, another truth of the matter was that the Sinterklaas in the spirit was very much alive and breathing. For Johnnie's father bought him a brand-new winter jacket with fur lining that felt so good a day before Christmas. It fell through the window as well because it, too, was unexpected. It became his favorite jacket.

But soon, the caravan left those environs. Trying for anything more of substance was like making oil and water act like bacon and eggs. It just didn't come together. Why? Even as an adult, Johnnie can't quite figure it all out. Somehow it wasn't one person's fault. It would be too easy to think that. It included choices made long ago, generations back. It was the two of clubs in every poker hand. It was nature and genes either gone awry or engaging in the survival of the fittest. It was the brokenness of life that visits and seeps into everyone, everywhere— the heart looking for the cracks of light in life. It was and is and is to come. Then came the Tet Offensive.

The Libyan Sybil

Culinary Red
Snaky Devil
Shoals of Grease
Heartache on Heartache
The Rainbow

Johnnie liked Play-Doh, punch-out stick-ons of Ruff and Reddy, and to his everlasting dismay—food colors. Especially the red, green, yellow, and blue dyes in the little, dark brown bottles with the dingy yellow labels on the top shelf of the cabinet in his mother's kitchen. Those little, dark brown bottles were a sensuous delight to his eyes.

One day, the red dye was left unattended on the kitchen table. Johnnie's mother had whipped together Johnnie's favorite red velvet cake for his birthday. She left the kitchen to dress to go buy groceries. It was such an exotic, inviting color that Johnnie thought it would be a good idea to paint the fake dog bone of Cyndy's. He was still trying to get Cyndy to play with him rather than growl. He felt the little brown Chihuahua would be more open to his overtures of friendship if Johnnie made her fake food prettier to chew on. So, he twisted the top off the dark brown bottle and proceeded to dab the fake bone with healthy amounts of this illicit delight. Well, in the heat of the moment, in walked Johnnie's mother. She was wearing her bedroom slippers, which explained why Johnnie did not hear her coming. Immediately, the red dye was confiscated from his hands like it was hot goods, the top twisted back on tight, and it traveled back to the top shelf of the kitchen cabinet.

A flow of words proceeded from Johnnie's mother that he would have rather not heard. Fortunately, the only shades of red in the kitchen, other than Cyndy's fake dog bone and the red velvet cake baking in the oven, were on Johnnie's mother's face, and not the kitchen floor or his backside. She made it painfully clear he was not to mess with any, any of the food colorings again, including the warm, fuzzy, blue one. She was out of sugar and needed to go to the grocery store to purchase more for the icing on Johnnie's birthday cake. He was not to let anyone in the house and again—especially, specifically, and most definitely—not mess with the food colorings. If he did, he would be in a whole heap of trouble and would not receive his birthday gift. He would "surely die," or words to that effect, if he even thought about "nibblin' on that piece of fruit" again.

At this point he reminded himself that Santa Claus was definitely out of the picture. Besides, she said there were "other trees in the garden" like his boy ventriloquist doll and choo-choo train that could occupy his time with enjoyment and pleasure. He was to stay in the den and not even take one step inside the kitchen. Thank you very much, slam, bang, and don't you forget it, and out she went to the store after changing her shoes.

The kitchen was next to the den. The boy ventriloquist doll was in Johnnie's bedroom taking an afternoon nap. The choo-choo train had a wheel missing. The room grew still.

"Mother shouldn't have left me without having a little bit of that red food coloring to play with. She knows I like colors and I like to paint," he thought.

He felt he had been led to water on a hot, thirsty afternoon and had not been allowed to take even so much as a sip of what now lay before him. He felt temptation. This time, it reared its beautiful, ugly head a little stronger than before because he was alone and nobody was looking. Again, he fancied. He heard something in the air singing like from the rocky shores of an island in the sea. Oddly enough it came from the top shelf in the now closed cabinet door in the kitchen. From the upper perches of that cliff on the kitchen counter isle came a hissing, enticing sort of melody that grew more alluring and louder.

"Play with me! Come play with me, Johnnie! It'ssssssssssssssssssss ssssssssssssssssssafe! It'ssssssssssssssssssssss okay. Sssssssssssssssssssshe won't mind."

"She won't?" Johnnie's heart asked.

"Why of coursssssssssssssssssse not, ssssssssssssssssssssshe loves you. You're the apple of her eye! Bessssssssssssssssssssides you have plenty of time before sssssssssssssssssssssssssssssshe returnsssssssssssssssssssssssss!"

And so he entered the kitchen.

He tiptoed over the blue linoleum tiles on the kitchen floor. When he landed at the kitchen counter isle, a problem presented itself. How was he to stand on the kitchen counter? How was he going to reach the object of his desire?

He wavered.

"Maybe I'd better go back," he thought as his head began to stir.

"Johnnie!" sang the food colorings with operatic gusto, especially the high tenor red one.

Oh, what to do? He just had to rescue those poor little dingy-brown bottles of food coloring from their captivity in the upper shelves of the kitchen cabinet.

"Okay, I'm coming!" shouted his unbridled, passionate heart that knew no via media.

"How do I get up on the counter?" he thought.

He looked around.

"The chair from the kitchen table, that's it!"

He pushed the chair over to the counter. In a hurried manner, for he knew that the "enemy" would be upon him at any moment, he scampered into the initial perch of his spaceship.

Standing on the counter, he looked out over the sea of blue linoleum tiles on the kitchen floor, to the deck of the den, to outside through the kitchen window next to the garage to see if there were any signs of trouble. While surveying the sky again, he heard the food colorings singing robustly, "Johnnie!"

"I said I'm coming!"

He leaned over to the cabinet door, ever so quietly tiptoeing, and carefully opened it. A whole forest of cans, bottles, and packages appeared before his eyes. Masses of stuff to eat, things familiar and things not so familiar, whose contents you might think twice about putting into your mouth. Items immediate and items at a distance in the shadows not fully known, receiving portions, thereof, echoes of true reality. So, like looking into a glass dimly, he only understood and saw in part. And through it all, toward the back of the shelf behind all of the known and unknown, sat the food colorings. Again, the temptation of unbridled passion swept over him, although he didn't know to call it that. He only knew by instinct that he just wanted that which lay within his grasp, and he wanted it now.

But then he paused. He contemplated the next step. He pondered the place before the place. He wondered the wages. He thought he heard a car in the driveway.

"Johnnie!" sang the food coloring bottles with rousing fanfare.

He looked out the kitchen window. The garage was still empty. He justified. He looked back at the driveway. He looked at the forlorn food colorings. He reached to pluck. And in the midst of his move, filled with ardor and desire, he lost his balance for a second. Just a second, mind you. Just one second. Just one itsy, bitsy, teeny tiny second. Oh, but the long interminable hours and hours and days and days of guilt and dismay that resulted from just that one little second. For you see, in the passion of the moment, as he was reaching with great haste and anticipation, his little left forearm connected to his little left wrist connected to his little left hand went awry in that second-filled chaotic moment, and knocked over a very fat mason jar with a rather flimsy, holey piece of aluminum foil wrapped over its top rather than a proper solid lid designed to keep the contents in.

But this was no ordinary mason jar. It was his mother's special Mason jar of syrupy, slimy, greasy, contents, filled chock-full of refuse from the previous frying of meats such as chicken, chopped steak, sausage, bacon, and—yuk!—liver. The jar had drippings and droppings from every sort of "once upon a time" animal in creation that found its way to Johnnie's house. Fatty materials galore abounded in the special mason jar of Johnnie's mother, in the days when calories and carbohydrates and fat grams and sugar grams and salt content were only talked about for the most part in special places like science classrooms and laboratories and among certain people who could converse with intelligence about such matters, before it became common knowledge to the masses of people with labels on food products that a common person could make a little bit sense out of.

These fatty materials were in a very liquid state of being. The leftover grease punctured the aluminum foil and flowed with abandon to the rear and the front and over the edge of the shelf, dripping down to the kitchen counter like one of those waterfalls Johnnie had seen in the National Geographic.

He placed the mason jar right side up. But this did little good since most of the greasy, slimy leftover drippings from countless chickens and livers from the past were out of the jar, discovering new territory, finding unseen corners, crevices, nooks, and crannies in the forest of cans, packages, and bottles. Areas that never had seen the light of day, areas that normally possessed a whiff of Lysol and Comet and glistened with a sanitized spic and span spit shine as a result of the incessant attention and elbow-grease Johnnie's mother, now underwent a transformation never before experienced in these environs. It was a washing of sorts.

Johnnie beheld these unfolding events. Stunned and in a state of semi-shock due to the rapid changes in his personal state of affairs, he tried to step down from the counter but to no avail. His feet slipped a bit this way and that, creating confusion and panic on his part. He went to his knees involuntarily and suddenly noticed a roll of paper towels by the sink, standing upright on the counter. The paper towels were beginning to resemble the leaning tower of Pisa due to the sweat of livers and chickens from bygone meals. Johnnie, who was also sweating by this time, grabbed the entire roll and proceeded to wipe as much as he could with broad sweeps across the top of the counter along with his own greasy hands, knees, and legs. This had the immediate effect of pushing the flowing grease even further out from its point of origin. The canisters of tea, flour, and sugar on the lower ends of the counter next to the toaster, along with the blue linoleum tiled kitchen floor, received the flood of dripping. It was justice rolling down like streams of water much to the dismay of Johnnie.

Back and forth went the roll of paper towels, this way and that went Johnnie's legs, hands, and knees, all working against each other trying to put things and matters aright before Johnnie's mother arrived on the scene. Suddenly Johnnie's chest and little chin found itself also involved in the wiping of the counter when his knees suddenly slipped out from under him. And in a twinkling of an eye and before the sound of the last trumpet, he slipped and landed with a resounding thump and bump on the blue linoleum tile kitchen flooded with grease drippings.

Johnnie looked toward the den and for the first time in their entire relationship, Cyndy stood within petting distance from him. She possessed a hint of smug satisfaction around the contours of her face. She, too, decided to join the fray and entered the kitchen. But her participation was short-lived. For as soon as she took one slide across the greasy kitchen floor that had the immediate effect of covering her little Chihuahua body and little Chihuahua feet with grease drippings, she decided enough was enough and ran as fast as her little Chihuahua legs could carry her back to the den, and for the first time in her entire stay, she jumped on the couch that Johnnie's mother and father watched Mr. Hitchcock's show from, instead of scooting back underneath the couch and out of sight. And also for the very first time, she started barking in that high-pitched, aggravating little Chihuahua way while wiping her greasy feet clean on the couch.

Then suddenly, Johnnie heard a car pull into the driveway. Everything grew very quiet, too quiet. Johnnie held his breath. Cyndy stopped barking, lifting and tilting her head in the air toward the driveway. There was a rustling of paper bags. The car door slammed. Cyndy began her high-pitched barking once more, except this time it was much louder and piercing. The food colorings were no longer singing their song.

The back door into the kitchen from the driveway opened. Cyndy went wild with barking from the den. Johnnie was on the floor with his greasy legs, feet, knees, and hands sprawled in every direction. He looked to the floor.

"Johnnie, what have you done!?"

He dared not look up. He could not look up. He had not heard that tone of voice before. But it was her, his mother. The grocery bags dropped to the floor.

"Oh Johnnie, what have you done? What have you done? Oh God, not today."

She spoke in a way he had never heard.

"Oh Johnnie…Johnnie."

He heard her walk carefully to the counter. He still could not look up. Cyndy stopped barking and ran to the entrance of the kitchen.

"Oh…"

She was whispering something he could not hear. She started crying.

He now became very aware of the grease as it seeped through parts of his clothing next to his skin. Its coolness made him shiver.

After what seemed like an eternity, she came to Johnnie. She helped him stand to his feet. The grease on his clothes soiled her white blouse. Her body was trembling. He dared not look into her face. Cyndy had disappeared.

While hovering over the welter and waste, she slowly took each article of his clothing off, a piece at a time. She was still crying softly.

When she completed undressing him, she walked him outside to the back yard. She picked up the garden hose, turned the spigot on, and doused him with water from head to toe. He still could not look into her eyes.

"Now, go to your sand box and get your bucket and shovel, and bring me some dirt, not the yellow sand. I want you to dig into the earth and bring me several buckets of the brown dirt underneath the grass and bring it back to the kitchen. I will be there waiting for you."

He walked to his sand box thinking, "Why did I do it? Why? Why?" He cried.

She was in the kitchen with a white towel to dry him off after bringing several buckets of dirt. She then scattered the dirt over the blue linoleum tile floor.

They ate supper in silence that evening. His father was off flying somewhere in a place called Vietnam. Cyndy was nowhere to be seen or heard.

There was no television. It was off to bed in short order. There would be a different bedtime story tonight, a different nocturnal prayer of sorts. As he got into bed, his mother walked into his bedroom with a second grocery bag. Not a word was spoken as she tucked him in. She sat on the edge of the bed and pulled out a brand new, shiny, beautiful watercolor set with a vast array of colors he had never seen before and genuine artist brushes of various sizes, and numerous brown pages of paper to paint on.

"For tomorrow," she whispered.

She got up, turned the lights out, and left the room, but her presence lingered on and on and on with the rays of the full moon shining into his bedroom window.

Mr. Chopin

Mr. John Thompson
Harvest Moon
Good Ole Boys
The Steep Mountain

Johnnie grew in some wisdom and in stature. He arrived at the calm plateau of his life, the span of time for several years before what fully being a human means comes to fruition and fruitfulness, before the imagination is stirred by an object causing a desire as one is trying to fall asleep. He arrived on this level plain where hills had been laid low after nine birthdays and continued through the twelfth. Johnnie still painted. Cyndy was long gone. Santa Claus had been found out. Afternoon naps were on a vacation. They would arrive back in a fury later in life.

It was during this era that another interest welled up from inside. The precise moment it started in the here and now he cannot say. It seemed to be always there. It was like meeting a stranger for the first time and feeling that you have known the person all your life. Its depths reached back beyond his earthly existence. It was with him, in the air. It suggested home, a peaceful garden. And one day it rose to the surface, on its own accord.

"Mother, I would like to learn how to play the piano," said Johnnie one afternoon.

She beamed. And some unknown number of days afterward, a piano arrived. He can still smell the fresh aroma of the new wooden black and white keys and the manner in which the dark brown, almost burgundy woodgrain glistened in the lights of the den as he played several random notes with one finger. He beamed.

And again after a number of days he can't be certain of, he began lessons with his male piano teacher and Mr. John Thompson and his *Teaching Little Fingers How to Play* book. It had a bright red cover. Inside the book, there were pictures of keyboards and hands, treble and bass clefs, sharps, flats, and natural signs, where notes landed on lines and spaces, where Every Good Boy Does Fine. No one had to beg, borrow, bribe, or steal Johnnie to sit in front of the keyboard. He did so voluntarily and joyfully. Time flew away; the only ticking heard was from a metronome on top of the piano.

His first recital was held at Christmas. The song he played was called "The Wigwam." Today, Johnnie can play the thirty-second piece without batting an eye. But then its length was more like a minute, although it seemed a thousand years to Johnnie, learning notes, and to his listening mother. At the Christmas recital, everyone was on edge. The only people who seemed to enjoy themselves were those who either did not have to perform or were not directly related to the performers.

For his efforts that evening, Johnnie received a miniature, plastic bust of Beethoven which to this day adorns his piano. Praises flowed after the event was over like the punch at the reception.

The number of "Sallys" far surpassed the number of "Johnnies" in such affairs, especially as their ages crept toward the teenage years and the pleasant nocturnal dreams, sometimes unasked for. Remember this was the early 1960s in American culture, or it should be more specifically said the early 1960s in Southern American Gothic culture. This place was south, way down south, of the enlightened world of Bach, Mozart, Beethoven, et al. It was so way down south that the deepest caverns knew very little in the way of preludes, nocturnes, etudes, and heaven forbid waltzes. If a growing boy talked about or even mentioned those terms and personages among relatives and acquaintances of the family, a nervous embarrassment grabbed hold and permeated the group gathered. It drew an enquiring look at the boy from a wondering, anxious relative or friend, or an amusing, almost sinister look from those who weren't really that close to the family or were anxious to articulate backhanded compliments.

A nondescript elephant had entered the room. Someone usually said something cute or catty or nonsensical or just plain downright stupid to break the awkward silence. An insincere laugh from the group gathered, followed with the immediate effect of getting the herd out of a predicament by injecting a subtle social commentary and avoid having to ponder too long the implications of a little boy's interest, especially a Southern little boy's interest, of those interests reserved only for little Southern girls. And furthermore, where was the football?

Looking back, Johnnie's mother cared for the right reasons for Johnnie's budding interest in the piano. She never said anything and never let it on that all that senseless chatter bothered her. Johnnie's father was usually off flying somewhere. As noted, Cyndy was history, so no editorial comment from those quarters. Johnnie continued learning to play the piano by tickling those ivories, memorizing their names by using both right and left hands, alone and then together, and in time played two notes at one time, creating chords. He progressed from "The Wigwam" to "Dona Nobis Pacem" and then to those waltzes by Mr. Chopin. He especially liked the "Minute Waltz," which he played in reality in front of his mother and in fantasy in front of thousands of people from all over the world in Carnegie Hall. He was also intrigued with what his piano teacher called the nocturnes of Mr. Chopin, those evening pieces that had a mystical calm, mixed quite suddenly with stirring outbursts like simmering flows of lava under latent volcanic rock.

Every time Johnnie heard a nocturne performed, even as an adult, he recalled a road trip taken with his parents. His father—in one of the few times he had both feet on the ground—was driving the car in the countryside late at night. His mother was seated next to his father on the front seat, scratching the back of his father's head. Johnnie was on the back seat leaning against a window, looking up at the dark sky with its countless stars and full harvest moon, hovering just over the horizon. Scattered clouds lit by the moon's glow hung in the night like wandering sheep in a pasture. All was quiet, except the hum of the car's engine. Nothing was stirring, not even Johnnie.

He wondered if Venus was somewhere in the crowd of clouds, for he had an overwhelming sense of peace. There was movement, a sort of dance among the elements, but it was silent. He looked at his mother and father and felt something about them that was beyond their being his parents. They were looking ahead, and what they were thinking he could only guess at. At the time, he did not know to articulate his feelings with words like that. But still, he felt it. He looked back at the glittering night sky. He wondered what was beyond the stars and the galaxies. The stillness and the shadows of the evening were serene. The steady forward movement of the car added to the sense of going not only to his present home, but also to another home far away.

Then suddenly what he saw stunned him. He stared. He dared not breathe. He looked to the dark car floor and then looked again up at the sky. It was not a dream. It was not a mirage. It was real. He blinked his eyes hard. It was still there. He also dared not say a word to his mother and father for fear that what he saw would disappear. The simple nocturne written by Mr. Chopin he was learning to play with his little fingers was playing in his head. He continued to look in amazement. The harvest moon was in its last stages, transforming its color from golden orange to a smaller orb of gleaming white. It was being embraced by an arm draped with flowing royal blue and crimson red robes, and a brown hand. The robe was layered fold after fold over itself as it extended the full length of the arm. In turn, the hand extended itself over the base of the moon. The eyes of the moon peeked over the arm—still looking—still hovering over the earth.

He stared for several minutes with rapt attention. The eyes were expressing something. Oh, Diana! And then the hand and arm slowly dissipated into the lazy puffing clouds, with wisps of its remains sailing upon the bosom of the air and then into the heavens. The car hummed forward.

He never forgot this moment. O blessed, blessed night. It was not a dream. It was substantial. Johnnie never doubted the encounter.

From that day forward, Johnnie and the moon had a secret pact between themselves, a knowing of sorts, an ongoing conversation. Stoney limits could not hold their love out. And in times of great ecstasy or perplexity or somewhere in between in Johnnie's life, it would call out his name, whispering, "Johnnie...Johnnie...Johnnie." He would look up, and the moon, in its fullness or in its slenderness or somewhere in between, would appear quite unannounced in the evening sky. Then it would slowly meander across the night sky, letting Johnnie know it was still there, hovering like an eagle over a nest of its young. The melody of a nocturne danced with the ethereal winds. It was a silver-sweet night. It was the sweetest sound.

The moon waxed and waned. It came and went full circle, at times not showing itself in its newness and at other times in its radiant full glory. At times love and life finding common ground.

As with everyone, there were momentary times of being part of the benevolent corporate. And then there was the camp of the herd at school, in particular, that held Johnnie in ridicule. He grew not in favor with most of his peers. It was with heavy looks he would go to school.

What was it in the Southern culture of good ole boys in the early 1960s that held, for the most part, the artistic boy in contempt, someone to rid the community of? Designated the outsider in school as Mr. Chopin came along for the ride? Looking back, Mr. Chopin, et al., were agreeable companions, mentors who guided and tutored him, and allowed him to keep his sanity, even though most had physically passed from the world stage. The polonaises, the waltzes, the etudes saw him through this vale of death's shadow. The public humiliations, the taunting, the spit wads on his back that came charging into his life were countered with the sweep of a chromatic scale or the romantic lilt of a melody. What would have happened to him otherwise?

Johnnie would often remember, even as an adult, one day standing in line outside his elementary classroom after recess, waiting to go back into the room. An odious peer of a boy possessing a World War II Nazi-Goering countenance, full of bravado and self-satisfaction in his face, stood behind him, whispering, "Johnnie," in a sickly tone of voice.

"I said, 'Johnnie.'"

"Yes," Johnnie turned around and looked at him as his classmates were lining up to go into the classroom.

Macho man looked him square in the face with no lighted glow, no presence of warmth and goodwill, no Hopkins-written "glassy white about the sky…and penciled blue so daintily." No, instead it reeked of a "darken'd landscape…the envied fruit with fatal smile." Johnnie looked into his dark brown eyes, cesspools.

"You're a sissy," he said.

"No, I am not," whispered Johnnie, turning away, looking toward the classroom door praying for the teacher to open it.

"Yes you are. Everyone says so."

"No, I am not."

The door would not open.

"Please, please open," prayed Johnnie.

"Yes, yes you are, you little sissy. You act like one. You are one. You're always playing jump rope with the girls. You little girl. You little sissy."

"Door open," pleaded Johnnie.

"Johnnie is a sissy. Johnnie is a sissy." Macho man sang the words in mocking, taunting, hateful rhythm.

Johnnie could hear several classmates behind Macho man start to giggle.

"Johnnie is a sissy!" Macho man said louder.

"God help me!" Johnnie panicked.

The classroom door opened.

Johnnie ran to his desk. He buried his head in his coat. It lay on top of the desk. It was the coat his father bought him the afternoon he told Johnnie the truth about Santa Claus. He cried. He heard voices all around, not daring to listen for fear of what they might be saying. Everything grew still. In front of the whole class, the teacher yelled out his name and told him to sit up straight in his chair. He was mortified.

"Johnnie is a sissy! Johnnie is a sissy!" rings that bell. Its tune, its rhythm, its sound etched in memory. It lives. It is passed on and on and on to the succeeding decades of his life to be met once again. It tries to grasp some meaning. It tries to discern. It tries to justify, to grab some sort of paradox that leads to something beyond and beneficent. Instead, like a malevolent boomerang, it returned to haunt.

"Good, very good, Johnnie," said the piano teacher.

That afternoon, Mr. Chopin arrived in the power and the glory through the music he had written, known as the preludes. Johnnie had taken to his piano and music and advanced at a rapid pace. When practicing at home, the tick tock of the clock was a stranger, the metronome its replacement.

"Now remember, let us hear the crescendo on the second and third beat of the measure shown by these two lines that start together at one point and then extend outward in opposite directions," said his teacher, pointing with a sharpened yellow pencil.

"Notice the lines travel apart until they reach the last beat of the measure. At this point the music is very loud, very dramatic. We need to hear and feel that. Have you ever been frightened by something or someone? Think about your response. Let us hear that in the music you create at this point."

Again his teacher pointed his pencil to the text.

"When the lines appear again on the next line, they start to come together. The music becomes softer. This is called a decrescendo."

The teacher drew squiggly lines under the word printed in the music.

"In this piece, the notes and the way they are played and the harmony of the piece returns us to a peaceful place, like being outside in the woods on a beautiful spring day. Even if we are the only ones experiencing it."

"Yes, sir," responded Johnnie.

"The music leaves that hateful moment and resolves back to a peaceful, major chord. It ends where it started. However, we feel differently about the ending than the beginning because of what we have just been through. And hopefully, if we experience another hateful moment, we will remember that, hopefully, we can return to that peaceful place."

"Yes, sir," repeated Johnnie.

"Now looking back at the point of the crescendo, we notice Chopin has written a B sharp and D sharp in the notes, so instantly the ear is aware of this struggle. Those two sharps unsettle us. They enter without warning. And when entering the mountaintop of the crescendo, just as suddenly and without warning, there is this romantic, wonderful melody, and the two sharps go away, although they do linger in the memory. Such is the genius of Chopin."

"Yes, sir," Johnnie said once again.

"Play the piece again. Be careful this time not to stumble over the sharps. Begin!"

Johnnie's fingers reached for the ivories. He felt a quiver of an intimate connection. Although at the time he did not know to articulate this feeling with such words, he did feel it in his bones. He did feel he was receiving the lifeblood of Mr. Chopin with his fingertips reaching out to Johnnie's fingertips. Mr. Chopin was there through the wide range of notes with dolce and andante, answering the question of how. The piano teacher's sharpened yellow pencil continuously guided Johnnie's eyes through the musical passage. At the same time, his piano teacher's breath smelled of fresh coffee.

Later that afternoon at home, Johnnie would practice the pieces on his piano. The music flowered and flowed through the open window of the room, sending its sounds across the hedges and grass, through the air, to the ears of the gardener raking the leaves in the front yard of Johnnie's teacher, giving the gardener a pleasant rhythm to work by, making merry his monotonous strokes and giving him a melody to whistle by, and in turn making the toil lighter. Johnnie was none the wiser as he played those two sharps and climbed the mountainous crescendo with its two sharps to the summit of a beautiful song proclaiming a peaceful existence.

New Frontiers

The Weeping Willow
The Muscadine Vine
The House in the Middle of the Woods
The Yellow Taxicab

J ohnnie moved to a new home at the age of twelve. He also started attending a new school.

His boy ventriloquist doll was laid away in a box covered with cloth and stored in the new attic. It was found fifty years later among his mother's things. The doll had kept the appearance of being brand new—a phoenix of sorts. Most noticeably, the television set with Mr. Hitchcock and the couch with the red spots remained behind as well. They all—including the growl underneath the couch—faded away into the past.

There was one lingering goodbye that was difficult to make. Several years before, a neighbor of Johnnie's had given him a weeping willow branch to plant. She told him to water it every day in its infancy, so it would live. He did. In time, the single slender stem grew into a taller, sturdier tree shooting forth long, slender branches with long, slender leaves hanging from its limbs: nature's canopy trophy, so graceful and serene that majestically withstood all kinds of weather. In Johnnie's departure, the encounter between the two was conducted with great dignity and a solemnity, reminiscent of graveside services.

As he stood saying goodbye, a light wind blew through and among the branches. The rustling of the hundreds of long, slender, leaves lightly sang their farewell. One long, slender branch swayed away from the group and gently brushed the face of Johnnie.

"Goodbye," said Johnnie.

"Goodbye," sang the weeping willow tree.

During the next few years, Johnnie's mother would drive him by the old house so he could say hello to his old friend. The tree grew and grew until it was quite large and majestic. Johnnie was proud to have had a hand in its being alive and flourishing.

Then one day they went by to visit. To their dismay, the tree was gone. A cheap, metal tool shed stood in his friend's place. He felt very empty and sad. An important part of his life had died.

"I wish I had taken a branch with me to plant at our new home. Oh, how I wish," he thought. He grieved.

"I am so sorry," said his mother.

"Me, too," he responded.

"Mother."

"Yes."

"I want to be called John now."

She paused and then said, "If you wish."

They drove back to their new home, never to return.

His new home had two stories. It was a brick house painted white with forest green shutters. There was a large front porch. One side of the house was referred to as a sunroom. It had straight glass slats at the windows. You turned a silver handle on the side to open them. Upstairs was John's bedroom. Across the hallway, his father, who was still gone a lot flying in skies all over the world, had a study, walled with dark pine wood panels with distinctive pine knots, across the hall. After his mother finished furnishing this room and when she had gone to the grocery store, he would open the door and peek inside. Many military citations, plaques, medals, and various memorabilia of his flights over Europe during World War II and Korea and other hotspots in the world hung on the wall, and from the ceiling hung model fighter planes in flight. He was afraid to enter for fear of disturbing something, fear of causing one of the planes to crash to the floor.

Downstairs, his parents had their own bedroom next to the living room where the piano found its resting place. Of course, practicing after supper was out of the question.

John liked being upstairs by himself. He could play and imagine new stories without much interruption. Even so, he would lock his bedroom door on occasion so no one would come in unannounced. He would pull out old toys and other objects to create a village located next to an active volcano, located on a tall chair with armrests. The toy soldiers and other figurines became characters in his drama. They would talk to each other, with him whispering the lines…until… the volcano erupted, the chair shook, and the village came tumbling down, with the main characters escaping on a boat cast out to the sea of his blue carpeted bedroom floor. Most of the time, he remembered to put the toys away after "The End." But every now and then, Rachel, the house cleaner who came twice a week, discovered his work. She would smile with a "what are you up to now" look and then proceed with her work.

John never grew tired exploring the house. There was always something new to discover, even in a room he had been in before. From the basement to the attic, he experienced the house in different ways. When in the basement, he could smell the damp, clay dirt. The boards would creak overhead when someone walked across the first floor. Spiders spun their webs in dark corners, knitting an intricate pattern with their spiny, black legs kicking thin, silky threads in mid-air. He imagined himself a spy for the government. In the attic, rather than hearing footsteps, the skittish sound of squirrels scampering across the roof to their nests, snuggled in open knotholes of the large oaks situated outside, spoke.

But what was most intriguing to John was the lay of the land behind the house. There were no cedar bushes to imagine space flights. Instead, there was a dense forest snuggled next to his and many other backyards in the neighborhood. The forest extended beyond the immediate horizon. It went somewhere mysterious, suggesting a strange, new world. A more swelling port of tall pines guarded its entrance. Draped around their trunks were wild muscadine and scuppernong vines running in every direction. John's mother explained to him that in the summer, large, tough-skinned grapes of regal blue and green would grow to be picked and eaten. John viewed the whole scene from his bedroom window. He painted pictures of the view with his watercolor set.

On the first Saturday morning in their new home, John felt inspired to explore his new frontier land at the end of his backyard to see what adventures might lurk, or what tree vines were waiting to be swung on.

While brushing his teeth before leaving the house, he heard a singular noise outside. It was like a knocking sound against a thick wooden door. He went to his bedroom window and looked out. To his surprise, he saw an elderly black man with a gray beard and moustache hoeing the ground at one side of the backyard. He was chopping and uprooting the undergrowth of crabgrass and other weeds.

Thud, thud, thud went the hoe.

John gazed at the man, who suddenly stood up. He turned and looked at John. He smiled a kind smile encased in a weathered face, his eyes sparkling in the sunlight.

John smiled, too, and haltingly waved. And for one brief instant, the man pointed at the forest and smiled once more. He then wiped his brow and continued hoeing.

John looked hard at the man. "I wonder if the man would like to travel with me into those woods," he thought. He wanted the man to wave again. He did not. And the funny thing about it for John was the longer he pleaded in his mind for the man to repeat his gesture, the more convinced he became that it happened.

John's mother was grocery shopping. As usual, his father was off flying somewhere in the world. Afternoon naps, as said before, had long ceased to exist. He now had a wristwatch to keep track of time. He decided, though, to write a note to his mother as to his whereabouts.

When John went out the back door, he saw that the man with the hoe had moved to the front yard.

John entered the forest through the row of guarding loblolly pines. It was a level place that spread many feet before him, with many paths converging in the area. He turned back and looked at his new home from a different vantage point. Much smaller but wider it looked.

Early muscadines were nowhere to be seen, nor was the poison ivy. His mother showed him pictures of the poisonous plant, warning him that it often lurked among other grasses and vines, posing with a posture of innocence and scarlet beauty. John looked up into the sky. He watched two birds circling in the air. He wondered whether Little Chirpy was in the air, alive and old enough to follow John to his new home.

Remembering the mighty oak tree with its majestic limbs placing him halfway to the moon, he wondered whether he would ever find such a tree again in this new frontier. He looked through the limbs of trees surrounding him to the reality of the heavens. Thin, finger-like clouds were penciled against the blue sky, skirting toward yonder crimson fireball drifting slowly downward toward the west away from John's new home.

He decided to follow the path toward the setting of the sun, its rays darting between two oaks and a pine. One of the oaks with low limbs had the makings of supporting a tree house. On he traveled. After meandering among bushes, the land descended into a clearing. Off to one side stood a singular, large shade tree. It was an oddity. It was the other in the midst of the status quo, a shining knight of peaceful intent, a sole shepherd in a frontier. Its knotty branches twisted and turned in every direction except the straight and narrow. Golden-green, heart shaped leaves draped the entire tree, flapping like fluttering banners in the wind.

John walked closer. A single leaf lay at its base. Picking the leaf up, he noticed its veins crawled in directions similar to those of the wrinkles in his hand—no discernable pattern, wandering veins some more pronounced than others. Yet the sum total of the veins composed its golden-green beauty. Then John noticed another oddity: dark-brown, long clusters of fruit dangling from the end of many leafy stems. Cigars came to John's mind. Cigars waiting to be plucked and puffed. John often saw his father smoke cigars. Ringlets of smoke would shoot forth from the mouth, as John's father tilted his head. This rite was performed in the backyard—rain or shine. John decided to take one of the tree's cigars home and try to do the same.

He walked to one of the lower limbs. He picked its fruit. He opened its dark-brown crusty shell. Countless papery-winged seeds flew into the air by circular winds. They were spirited about in random fashion; it was vain trying to guess where the seeds fell. Following one covey dancing just above the earth, he stumbled into another new thing: rows of unkempt plum bushes, congregating together. Planted in another era, this source of preserves fed only the birds and a wandering boy. Savoring the flavor of the tender flesh in his mouth, John ate his fill while walking up and down the rows with outstretched arms and hands brushing against the bushes.

He looked back at the shepherd tree, marveling at its faithfulness at watching the plum orchard no matter how the world changed. Its solid strength spoke, saying contra mundum, contra mundum, contra mundum. Its dancing limbs warned against violating what this frontier stood for, its essence at this moment.

Yonder crimson fireball was descending farther and farther into the canopy of oaks, maples, and pines. Its twinkling, darting rays were colored in a rose-pinkish tint. John felt an invitation extended to walk out of the plum orchard and farther away from his new home.

Shades and shadows lengthened as the soil proved damp enough to sprout blankets of ferns in every direction. He walked through the multitude of fronds. The petite leaves were so delicate, so intricately designed. It was a much older area of the forest. Horses and carriage wheels graced their presence nearby once where John now walked with caution in the stillness—afraid of disturbing whatever peace may have found a home. An eternal connection to all that had been and to all that will occur permeated his soul. He could smell and hear the earth—*adamah, adamah, adamah.* Years later, he would reflect on this passageway and still was not able to adequately articulate the experience.

A sparrow sang. Its voice startled John. He ran farther westward. Without warning, he stumbled onto a dirt road, managing a leap over the ditch gracing the road's borders at the last second. Stopping to catch his breath and balance, he looked in both directions that the road lay. At one end, way off, he saw cars fleeting by in both directions. Most of the windows and metal bodies of the cars were catching the glimmers of the late afternoon rays of the sun and reflecting them back toward John like mini laser beams. At the other end of the road, he saw the front of an old, dingy, two-story, dull white Victorian house with a wraparound porch on both levels. At the front entrance, there were two massive, Doric columns gracing the entrance like sentinels of a fort. Wisteria hung from the upper balconies. The thick forest of oaks, maples, and pines draped the house on the sides and up the dirt road on both sides where John stood. The trees blocked any further view of what lay beyond. He decided to get a closer look at the house. Besides, the road would take him back in the direction of his new home, sort of.

As he walked toward the house, the squish, squish, squish sound of his footsteps on the soft, orange dirt on the drive seemed to be shouting his approach. He stopped and looked around. All was still. A slight breeze stirred in the trees. He waited. No sound was coming from the house. He started walking once more, and squish, squish, squish went his feet.

He approached the point where the dirt driveway circled behind the house to the left. He stood transfixed. The windows were tall and narrow. There was darkness inside the house—nothing seemed to be stirring. Majestically it stood with a grand silence that spoke of a bygone era of farmers, model T's, and cows lowing in the surrounding fields.

An elegance gone shabby, yet its glory days were still shining through; a bustling past whispered about. Cackling of hens, crowing of roosters, and the grunts of hogs heard in imaginative circles of John's mind.

John felt welcomed.

Suddenly, he heard the sound of a car motor behind him in the distance. He turned. He saw a yellow taxicab coming his way. Without thought, he dashed into the woods, ran a short distance, and hid behind an overgrown boxwood bush. His heart was pounding in his chest.

The yellow taxicab slowly approached. It stopped in front of where John was hiding. An elderly lady with short gray hair and wearing a mink-laced pink hat and a white scarf around her neck was seated in the back seat. She peered out at John through the dusty window. She wore thick-lens glasses, making her eyes seem all-seeing and all-knowing. The crevices in her face streaked in all directions.

John studied her face through the openings in the boxwood bush. She turned her head and stared right at him, as though there was no boxwood bush. He froze. Her gray, almost light blue azure eyes revealed a glazed glassiness of what seemed to him a profound annoyance.

The dusty passenger window of the yellow taxicab began to descend, squeaking and rubbing against the metal in the door at intervals. Haltingly it went down, not quite on track. The elderly lady moved her face forward out of the taxicab. She peered at John. John stared back. He was frightened stiff. She placed her right, gray-gloved hand at the base of the door's window.

"What are you doing here?" she shouted.

John did not dare to say a word.

"Don't pretend you are not there. I can see you!"

John knew for sure she could. It seemed the whole world grew still. The birds had stopped singing. The taxicab driver turned the motor off. She continued gazing into the woods at John.

Then suddenly she turned to the taxicab driver and screamed, "Get him, he's a trespasser!" She lifted her gray-gloved hand and pointed out the window.

The taxicab driver opened his door.

And like a wild rabbit frightened out of his hiding place, John took off running into the forest at lightning speed toward his new home. Never had he run so fast. Some unexpected force kicked in. Leaves and branches flew past. Swish, swish, swish went the low-lying branches and undergrowth, as he leapt over a fallen pine tree and sped past a vine lounging against an old oak tree. He took no notice of the Shepherd tree or the plum orchard. He flew into the level place in the woods, raced through the guarding pines and into his new backyard.

He saw his mother talking to the black man with the gray beard. She was kneeling on the ground with her back to him, but the man saw John coming out of the new frontier. He smiled at John. John instantly brought one of his fingers to the lips for him to keep silent. The man responded in like manner, while John's mother continued looking at the ground, talking without noticing the exchange.

John sprinted to the opposite side of the new house and entered through the front door. He immediately went to the kitchen. The note was exactly where he left it. It appeared to have been unobserved. John grabbed the note, dashed upstairs, slammed his bedroom door, scurried into a closet to hide, and tore the note into many pieces.

John and Matilda

The Blue Bloods
I Wanna Hold Your Hand

"You're new here, aren't you?"
"I used to go to another school, and then we moved into a new house near here."

"What's your name?"

"John."

"My name is John, too. Which sports do you like?"

"None really. I've never played much."

"Why?"

"I don't know why?"

"Do you want to play?'

"I can't. I don't really like it."

"What do you like?"

"I like to play the piano." *Oops, it slipped*, thought John.

John looked at John with a smirk. The veteran John of the school kicked the dirt, dust flying everywhere. He started laughing and then ran off toward a group of boys huddled in the corner of the playground. It was recess. John had been at the new school for one day. He was in a huge field of boys and girls laughing and playing. They congregated in pairs, small or even larger groups playing chase or kickball. The rookie John stood alone.

It seemed most of the class had been going to school together since day one of first grade. And on top of that, the kids carried a certain air about them. It was the way they held their heads, talked, and signaled to each other as to who was in and who was out. The kids were the noblesse oblige, the crème de la crème, the up-and-coming, the heirs apparent—some even trust fund babies—of the town. Blue bloods, if you will. The third, fourth, and in some cases fifth generation of the pillars of the community families with prestige, money, and power. Streets were named after this group—even the school was. These kids lived in really nice homes with lots of ivy growing on them—beautiful gardens with a kaleidoscope of colors. Their homes weren't brand spanking new like John's. Their yards looked like the Augusta golf greens, whereas John's yard was more reminiscent of Death Valley. Green grass was still offstage.

However, the elderly black man whose skin shone a melanin shine was working to change that. The flower garden was beginning to bear fruit. His name was Mr. Jesup. These kids' grandparents lived in really, really nice homes. They traveled to Europe on occasion. The kids also had older brothers and sisters who offered assistance on the science fair projects. John made do with the World Book Encyclopedia.

At that age, whenever John heard the word "class," he thought only of school, not a social system. But the reality of the class reflected the reality of the class beyond the four walls of their classroom. The "inner ring" sat in chairs around John. He was none the wiser, yet he detected a whiff of privilege permeating the air. "Deference" was also a word that was a stranger in John's vocabulary until he was an adult, and then he encountered it only once in a blue moon. With deference the inner ring blue bloods treated each other and the teachers treated them, and deference was evident in how the principal acted whenever he was patrolling the area, and round and round it went come rain or shine, every day, all day unless it was the weekend, holidays, or no school days when teachers were given some time off to regroup. John felt these things but was never able to put words on it. As implied above, his vocabulary was limited.

In short, he was the new kid on the block, trying to construct a "new" John whom people would like. But as he discovered, playing the piano was not a favorite pastime for the boys. Their fathers seemed to all have their jobs downtown on Main Street, whereas John's father was making lots of "new" money flying all over the world, especially over a place called Vietnam, which people were beginning to hear about more and more. He was having a hard time.

And so, there he stood, alone on the playground during recess. However, there was another boy off to himself. In later recesses, they communicated some. Something stirred in John when he was around him. Some emotion with wings and an arrow. The boy was a year younger and "new," as well. The last time John saw him, they put their arms around their respective shoulders as they walked back to their respective classrooms. This felt right and good to John. They smiled to each other as they parted. But something happened. The boy never appeared again on the playground. The next day, John stood alone once more. He sat in the dirt. He wept. The bell rang. Recess was over.

Culture appreciation was next on the agenda for the day. John liked culture appreciation, especially when the teacher read stories about "The Swamp Fox." John possessed an admiration and affinity for the lifestyle of the revolutionary. There was a certain romance about the whole thing, although he didn't know to think in those terms at the time. Living in the woods, evading the snooty British with their taxes and highfalutin accent that always made them sound smart, even if what they said was the dumbest thing in the world. It was an earlier Frontier Land for adults, which gave John some hope for the future.

So he would sit quietly listening to his teacher who reminded him of his grandmother. She read with a regal, lower state brogue from the coast. She would begin by letting out a loud "ahem," which was a signal for no more talking. Next, being a bit overweight, she would hoist herself up on the stool. Her head would cock itself in a certain position toward the windows of the room. Then words heralded forth from her mouth, with each syllable enunciated distinctly, especially the ones that ended with the letter "t." Then there were words like "boat" and "about" that she would pronounce in a funny sort of way.

At certain exciting climaxes, she would pause for dramatic effect, gazing out the classroom windows. In a twinkling of an eye, it was though she was riding with the Fox, chasing the dratted British, leaping over hedges into the swampy morass of mud and water, dodging flying bullets. Thirty-nine children and John sat there transfixed, listening with bated breath as to what would happen next and who would survive the terrible ordeal that faced the men of the Swamp Fox. John sat dreaming up stories inspired by what he was hearing. He planned to act out what he imagined behind his new home later that afternoon.

On one memorial culture appreciation day, as she was hoisting herself on the stool, a loud seismic crack sounded in the room. A sudden silence descended never before heard. Not missing a beat, the teacher stood suddenly at attention and roared forth with orders for the troops to descend on those who would tax without representation. In a flash, she grabbed the stool, brandished it like a sword, and then swung it into the wall next to her desk where it proceeded to splinter and splatter into many pieces. The children were spellbound. No one hardly breathed, and forty expressions of amazement and awe shone as bright as the rising sun on a clear morning. The class was forever moved. For John, his teacher forever transformed herself from a resemblance of his grandmother to the Mr. Brownlow of Oliver Twist that he was at the time enthralled with. And when he read the next chapter of the escapades of Oliver that evening, when Mr. Brownlow appeared, he, too, possessed a regal, lower state brogue from the coast.

One day, the teacher was out of town. Instead there was a substitute. So culture appreciation was assigned to one of the girl students by the teacher several days prior. The class was told to share something about present day culture, something of significance to the world, something of worthwhile distinction that uplifted the human spirit, and so on and so forth.

The student was named Matilda. John's perceptive, intuitive antennas were developing quite nicely, growing in wisdom to the point that he knew by instinct Matilda was for all intents and purposes not one of the blue bloods. He wasn't totally sure, but if he had been a betting boy, he would have said most likely Matilda was a newcomer as well. Later he found out that she was indeed, having started one year before John. She hung around two other girls who were sullen, silent types, wearing horn-rimmed glasses. One had buck teeth; the other wore braces. They bore the hushed scorn from some of the bluer of the blue-blooded girls.

John found out that the mates of Matilda had attended the school since first grade. They were relegated to the outer ring of society from day one. Their respective families lived not far from the school in a slither of a neighborhood that contained more modest homes than the surrounding community. When Matilda arrived the year before, however, social matters started changing and shook the expected up. Matilda was like the second rooster in a flock of hens. She took these two compatriots under her wings. They started coming out of their shells.

Consequently, matters were always on edge with the girls in general, especially after becoming educated to the exploits of the Swamp Fox. There was a constant electric tension in the air, where the least spark might set off a fiery explosion. And since the boys, for the most part, hated girls at this age, they would stand back and watch in a bemused silence. Matilda was also bigger and taller than any girl in the class. Her dresses never quite fit. They had a whiff of hand-me-downs about them. Her flaming red hair was cropped. She never smiled but instead wore a scowl. Her hand was always in a balled-up fist position, ready to punch the face of any smart a--. It was rumored that her mother was living with a man who was not her father. And on top of all that they were Yankees from up North.

"Class! Class! For the last time don't talk so much. Matilda! Come share with us!" pontificated the substitute teacher.

Matilda slowly rose from her seat. She approached the front of the class stealthily like a great lion in the fields of Africa with an eye on some dinner. In her hand was a 45-rpm record.

"I need the record player," murmured Matilda.

"What did you say? I don't understand you," responded the substitute teacher.

"I said I need the record player!" yelled Matilda.

The class grew quiet. In one sentence Matilda accomplished a silence from the class that the substitute teacher was never able to bring about the whole day.

"Oh, how nice. We're going to listen to some music, class! John (this was the blue blood John), would you bring the record player from the back and set it up for Matilda like a nice little boy?"

John kicked the floor and then proceeded with the assignment.

"And class, please, I know your teacher would appreciate it if you told her you would need extra equipment ahead of time, so we won't be sitting here with nothing to do!"

Matilda's face transformed itself into a much deeper scowl than she usually carried. John set the record player up. Before leaving, he mimicked the scowl on Matilda's face to the class. That act caused an outburst of laughter from most of the kids, indicating their approval, with the exception of Matilda's two sidekicks and the "new" John.

"Class! Class! John, let's don't be so incorrigible," said the substitute teacher in a deferential manner. Nobody understood what she said, even the blue blood girls, but everyone stopped laughing just the same because Matilda turned and faced the class herself with seething anger.

John kicked the floor and sat down.

"Matilda, what piece of music do you have to share with us today?" asked the substitute teacher.

"'I Wanna Hold Your Hand'!"

"What!?" screamed the substitute. There was another outburst of laughter, although a little more subdued this time.

"Class!"

Snickers reverberated through the room.

"Class!"

Silence reigned.

"What did you say, dear?"

"'I Wanna Hold Your Hand,' that's the name of the song."

"Oh, who is it by…dear?"

"The Beatles."

A few giggles erupted.

"Class! Who?"

"The Beatles. They were on the Ed Sullivan show the other night."

"Ah yes, now I know who you are talking about, dear. The Beatles are those nice-looking boys from England who need a haircut."

"I reck-an," said Matilda in a mocked low country Southern accent.

"Matilda, 'reckon' is probably not one of the best of words to use when speaking in public."

Matilda scowled back at the substitute, who pretended not to notice as she hoisted herself up on the new culture appreciation stool.

"You may play your piece of music, dear," said the substitute.

Laboriously, Matilda put the 45-rpm on the spin table, turned the switch on, and placed the needle on the outer groove, spinning around and around. What she did not know and what she and the substitute and the rest of the class were momentarily going to discover was that blue blood John when setting up the record player not only plugged the chord into the wall socket, but also with a slight sleight of hand, turned the volume knob up to the loudest position it could go. So when the Beatles started their song with "Oh I…," not only were Matilda and the class able to hear the piece of music, but so were several of the adjoining classrooms down the hall.

The resultant blast and blare caused the class, particularly the blue bloods, to roar with laughter because of the noise and the added pleasure of seeing Matilda jump out of her skin, which looked to the class, particularly the blue bloods, like an attempt to do the "twist," and at the same time seeing the substitute descend from her perch on the new cultural appreciation stool in a most unladylike Southern fashion and grabbing Matilda's right hand as both stumbled face forward toward the floor.

But even grabbing Matilda's hand in a desperate move did not prevent bringing the substitute to her knees. Fortunately, Matilda and the substitute teacher's fall was broken by a student's strategically placed desk, but the books and loose papers on top of the desk flew off in every direction. The substitute was on the same level as the class with the climatic result of seeing the teacher's head bob up and down in her attempt to regain a culture appreciation composure. Matilda went all the way to the floor.

The class went wild. The girls were screaming with orgasmic abandonment like the ones on the Ed Sullivan show, as the boys were boisterously laughing with equal out of tune enthusiasm, straining harsh discords and unpleasing sharps. Charity was a stranger as original sin and Mother Nature gained the upper hand.

The long and short of it was "I wanna…" never progressed to "I did" for anybody. That last electric guitar strum from the song never found its voice in the class. Those particular singers on that particular stage never found those particular lights in that classroom setting again. In fact, when the principal found out about all the mayhem, music written less than fifty years ago was banned from culture appreciation from that day on. Even Rachmaninoff was considered raunchy. Recent musical expressions were sent to the outer rings of social oblivion. 45s were not allowed in, and if seen, would be immediately confiscated. The line between the blue bloods like the other John and the red bloods like Matilda was drawn a little deeper in the sand that day. It grew deeper and deeper as the class moved on in the years ahead to junior high and high school. And it took a drunken graduation party out in the middle of the woods seven years later to find a sliver of a crack in that wall. So John was told.

The merciful end of the day bell rang before the administration descended. John left with his books in tow. He, Matilda, and her two buddies left subdued. Matilda forgot her record.

John wandered off by himself, wishing his newfound friend was around. His mother was late picking him up, so he walked over to the baseball field. Suddenly, he noticed he had left a book he was reading on his desk in all the chaos. It was Enid Blyton's *The Castle of Adventure*. He loved the characters and story. The chapter he read the previous evening had ended with a cliff hanger, and he was anxious to find out what happened next. So back to the classroom he went.

It was very quiet and still as he approached. He walked toward the side backdoor into the classroom. As he climbed the outdoor stairs, he could hear music being played very softly. Before entering, he peeked inside the room. At the front of the classroom sat the substitute in a student's chair. The record player was positioned on top of the new culture appreciation stool. The substitute was crying listening to "I Wanna Hold Your Hand." Her face was looking out the window with an expression of enormous sadness.

John quietly turned and left. He felt sad. His heart went out to the substitute teacher. He would have to wait to find out what happened in the next chapter of his book. He vowed that he would always respect substitutes in the future. In a funny sort of way, they were as much an outsider as he was. And yet, in the years ahead for the class, there was an ever-increasing waxing and waning of the idea that they were all people made of one blood. In their own and wider world, the eternal movement between fear and love was seen in a mirror, darkly.

John felt the soft sand under his feet as his mother pulled up in her car. The substitute was never seen again. John wondered occasionally what the next chapter in her life was like.

The Food of Love

The Brick Closet
Mr. Beethoven
Breaths of Silent Taunts

Seventh grade, with its attendant ways and means, was the best and the worst of times for John. It meant the changing of the guard—new students from other elementary schools entered—and the changing of classes for the first time. There was something promising, yet threatening, about the whole set up. The promise was attending a band class. The threat was having to dress out for gym.

John continued to construct his new persona, plank by plank, brick by brick. Yet the façade did not change his interior self as much as he wanted it to. The outer covering, in fact, was smothering or at least hampering his soul. Yet the seeds of a much future blossoming did take root in his case. In time, the day would come when boards would rot and ivy would sprout, climbing up a brick wall, which in time would begin cracking the brick and mortar.

Part of this state of affairs was due to the benevolent influence of Mr. Jesup, who tended the yard every fortnight. After school, he and John would talk and talk and talk about everything and anything. John did most of the talking, while Mr. Jesup hoed, planted, trimmed, and grinned, and then in a most pleasing and sonorous manner added some wit and wisdom at the end of a story. And then when the conversation lulled into silence, Mr. Jesup would suddenly say, "John, go play something for me on the piano while I work."

"Sure," and off John went, making sure the windows were open so Mr. Jesup could hear the latest piece of music he was learning to play.

It was during seventh grade that Mr. Beethoven joined company with Mr. Chopin at John's keyboard. The unsettling turbulence of Mr. Beethoven quickened John into moods and emotions stirring within himself that felt...well...human. But Mr. Chopin was not to be outdone. For soon enough, John's piano teacher escorted The Revolutionaire into the repertoire. And then, not to be outdone in the versatility front, in a rejoinder, along came "Fur Elise," written by Mr. Beethoven. So there was this pulsating, ebbing and flowing force that kept John moving and breathing.

All the while, John continued constructing the castle around himself. Fortunately, solid rocks were mixed in with the sand in the foundations. Band joined hands with gym. Art joined hands with algebra. Running in the mule train in gym was an absolute terror. Learning to play the clarinet in band was a sheer delight. Formulas and proofs turned minutes into hours, while painting a bird's nest in a tree was like traveling through time at lightning speed.

The bulk of community in seventh grade became less articulate as to John's position in that society. But the echoes remained of what he had experienced before. Taunts, if not spoken out loud, were muttered under breaths. There was always lying in wait, always ready to pounce, at the least perceived provocation like striking out at bat or not wanting to take a shower, the hatred or intolerance as to who John was. But community also chose John as first chair clarinet in band and also offered more sustained applauses at the end of solos at recitals. His first year, he received a small, plastic bust of Mr. Bach's head, which joined Mr. Beethoven's. Embracing and keeping the whole situation in check were the church John attended on Sunday morning and his talks with Mr. Jesup.

John kept hammering away on all fronts. The walls were becoming quite sure of themselves. But the workmanship was not of a superior quality, because loose tiles and cracks between joists abounded as the seeds continued sprouting away.

Christmas

A Dark Brown Coin
The Tet Offensive in Vietnam
The Telegram

John's father was home for Christmas and the New Year. Looking at everyone and everything was a concentrated effort on his part. He was unfocused to the point of an awakened faraway focus of something more dreadful, mysterious. Smoking cigarettes one after another in front of a new blank television screen was a daily activity in the mornings. At meals, conversation was of a perfunctory tone. And since John now knew all about Mr. Santa, no references were made to the upcoming visit. There was a tree and there were modest gifts.

One morning John walked into the den and sat across from his father.

"They say we're winning," said John's father without looking at John.

"Good," responded John.

"Yeah," said his father.

They sat for a few minutes in silence.

"Oh, by the way, before I forget. I brought you back something. Here," said John's father as he pulled a dark brown coin out of his pocket.

"Thank you," said John.

"You can't ever spend it here on anything. Not even a candy bar."

"Why?" asked John.

"Because it's Vietnamese money."

"That's okay."

"Think of it as a good luck charm. Here, let me kiss it."

John's father leaned over and kissed the dark brown coin. He traced his finger over John's hand.

"Lucky money?" asked John.

"Yes, lucky money," whispered John's father. He took a deep drag on his cigarette.

That evening, during the middle of the night, John heard screams from downstairs. At first, he was afraid of getting out of his bed. Then he heard some movement in the main hallway. He quickly got out of bed to find out what happened. As he started to descend the stairs, his mother came quickly from side door of the kitchen.

"What's wrong mother?"

"Nothing dear, go back to sleep. Your father had a bad dream."

"Can I help?"

"No, go back to bed; he'll be all right. We'll see you in the morning."

When John was getting dressed the next morning, he looked out his bedroom window and saw his father talking to Mr. Jesup. They were standing by the flower garden. Mr. Jesup was showing his father some odd-looking bulbs. They were laughing and talking as Mr. Jesup made gestures with his hands and occasionally referred to the bulbs. For the first time since coming home, John's father was smiling while puffing away on a cigarette and at the same time, reaching inside his pocket. He pulled out a dark brown coin. It looked the same as the one he had given John. He gave it to Mr. Jesup. They talked for a few minutes. Then they shook hands. John's father walked back into the house.

John's father left for Vietnam the next day.

Several weeks later, John watched the rising moon from his bedroom window. He thought about the time he saw the hand and arm embrace the moon some years before. His father had been driving in silence in the countryside. He had been in the back seat. Nothing but the celestial brightness had embraced their journey home. John went to his desk drawer to look at the dark brown coin given by his father. Picking the coin up, John went back to his bedroom window. He felt sad but felt a singular contentment while gazing at the moon. The clouds were effortlessly smoking around and about in the skies. He felt his father. He felt his father's hand tracing his hand. Then everything was dark and still.

January 30, 1968

In February, John's mother received a telegram from the Air Force saying that it regretted to inform her that her husband was missing in action. It was early evening. John was in his bedroom painting. He heard his mother scream from downstairs.

Feast of Flowers

The Beige Envelope
Aunt Jules
Missy

"Yes, ma'am, yes, ma'am, I hear you," said Mr. Jesup to John's mother.

John was at an open window overhead listening. He heard the soft murmur of his mother's voice. He looked out the window and saw Mr. Jesup standing still outside the back door.

John heard a sparrow screeching from a tree limb. A cat was slowly meandering underneath the bird.

"I could. I could do that," said Mr. Jesup.

John could not make out what his mother was asking him. She sounded despondent. Her voice was broken. He imagined tears.

The back screen door was slightly ajar. His mother's hand was extended, shaking the hand of Mr. Jesup. She stepped out of the house and hugged Mr. Jesup. She then handed him a long, beige envelope. The sparrow screeched louder.

"I'm sorry this is necessary," she said nodding to the envelope.

"Winter is a passing, it's a passing," he intoned.

She walked over to the bed of flowers. Bending over, she gathered a bunch into her arms—a kaleidoscope of colors wrapped in the early mint tones of recent budding of green leaves. She walked back to Mr. Jesup and placed the bouquet in the nook of his arms.

John walked away from the open window. He heard the screen door slam shut.

Mr. Jesup shooed the cat away. The sparrow followed the cat overhead, circling and darting in mid-air. Mr. Jesup walked toward his truck, murmuring from his beloved Longfellow, "And the mother gave, in tears and pain, the flowers she most did love; she knew she should find them all again, in the fields of the light above."

Mr. Jesup hopped into the truck. He placed the flowers on the passenger side of the front seat. He started the engine. While moving down the gravel road, he started humming "Lead On, O King Eternal."

"Now, John, you listen to me. You must obey Mr. Jesup. You must do everything he tells you to do."

"Yes, ma'am."

"No wandering off."

"Yes, ma'am."

"No back talk or smart remarks. I've given him strict instructions to let me know if he has any trouble with you. He knows where I will be. He knows how to contact me. Last I checked the U.S. Postal service and the telephones are still working."

"Yes, ma'am, I hear you."

John's mother sat on his bed.

"I'll be down to meet you as soon as everything is taken care of here," she whispered.

"Mother?"

"Yes?"

"Is Aunt Jules nice?"

"Nice? Well, yes and no. She's older than me and she means well. She has never been cruel but is determined about things she cares about, to see they are done right. So you won't be able to do anything you like. I have always looked up to her. She has what I call a shining quality that I never had. She draws people in and out. Dismantles any walls they may have. And she can tear up a piano without a lick of music in front of her. Ask her to play the boogie woogie."

"Why can't I wait and come with you?"

A truck horn started blowing outside.

"There's Mr. Jesup. Bring your suitcase. Did you get some of Mr. Verne's books to read?"

"Yes, ma'am."

"Let's see—*Around the World in Eighty Days*. I think that might be appropriate. Come on, we mustn't keep him waiting."

"That's my little man," thought John's mother, looking out the bedroom window as the engine of Mr. Jesup's truck started to rev into action. "Oh the pain, the pain of those twenty-four hours from my little man—wouldn't believe it looking at him now. You certainly didn't want to leave me. I must have fed you really good. Oh, the cutting pain. You hurt me so much. I thought I was going to die. I can't believe it even happened, seeing how you turned out. Only when you leave me do I think about it. When he gets out of sight, he won't kick so hard for me to love him. But…but…the pain has never really gone away. The cord still pulls. It hurts. It will never be cut, Johnnie. I'll join you soon."

John's mother ran down the stairs and out the front door.

"Good-bye!" she shouted.

Mr. Jesup looked at her along with John.

"Good-bye," said John, waving his hand limply several times.

"She can't let go, no sir, she just can't let go," thought Mr. Jesup, smiling.

John sat still. He was looking at the floorboard. He was thinking. He wanted to get rid of "it" as he said good-bye, but didn't know how, because he hadn't figured out what "it" was he wanted to get rid of. Maybe getting rid of "it" was too strong a feeling, maybe just put "it" aside—that's it put "it" aside. He felt a drag, something holding on to him, that he wanted to cut loose, but didn't know how. He felt sleepy about it, and he wasn't sure he wanted to cut loose, yet he wanted to. It was a terrible feeling. John had a headache.

"Ready, John?" asked Mr. Jesup.

"Yes sir," he replied.

John looked out the windshield and began waving to his mother once again.

"They're still wavin'," thought Mr. Jesup, "They've had more than enough time. I need to floor ole missy a little. Rev her up, yes sir. Get some distance between those two."

Mr. Jesup backed rather quickly out onto the street.

"Come on, Missy," he whispered.

"Bye!" yelled John.

"Carry us down this road through shoals and tides. Let's head to flower land!" cried out Mr. Jesup.

"He's speeding, and he's never done that before. Never, never, never! I ask you, Mr. Jesup, why?!" John's mother said aloud.

She thought about looking up to the skies and shaking her fist but dared not. That cord seemed stretched, though, and she felt the pain, oh the cutting pain. It was thinning out like a spider's thin wisp of a thread, dangling away from the heart of things. She wanted to twitch that thread back to her but realized the futility at this point.

She looked around. No sounds. Birds were quiet. All of a sudden, she felt a numbing loss. She felt queer. Whom did she really know, including herself?

She looked across the street. Bright blue blinds were hanging in the windows of the house. She saw two of the slats bend. A small, dark opening appeared. She could not see anything. She felt the urge to wave and acknowledge the presence of whoever it was spying on her. She had never met these neighbors. "Now, it really doesn't matter," she thought. "I'll be out of this neighborhood shortly. I bet they don't even realize what has just taken place—oblivious to my little Johnnie having gone away. But that is okay, because I will be his mother—always. Trucks scan speed away, little boys can go to Florida, husbands can disappear in Vietnam, but I will always, always, be his mother."

She felt a little uneasy but at the same time not quite alone. The slats snapped back into place. She walked back toward her house, realizing life was still pulsating elsewhere regardless of how she felt at this moment.

She climbed the front porch steps. She turned. She waved. She entered her home to begin packing.

Missy sped on down the road. Thus, the longest journey John had taken began. To the Feast of Flowers, the Pascua Florida—Florida, the land of sun and oranges and musical towers. It was there that John and Mr. Jesup would journey.

Part II

The Woodpecker Trail

Alphaburg
Orange Crush
Zion

Mr. Jesup looked over at John. The boy sat silently looking out his window.

Mr. Jesup knew he was silently crying. They had been traveling for two hours.

"He's lost a lot," thought Mr. Jesup. "Yes, sir, he's lost a lot."

They were traveling through the last vestiges of cotton fields and approaching a small town before crossing the Savannah River into Georgia.

"Alphaburg, three miles," said Mr. Jesup.

John did not respond.

"I need to get that boy to open up," thought Mr. Jesup.

"What day is this, John?" asked Mr. Jesup.

"…Wednesday, I think. Why?"

"Yep…just wanted to make sure," replied Mr. Jesup.

"Mother said I was born on a Wednesday. She said I wasn't in a hurry to get here."

"Yep…it's a tough world to wanta climb into."

They drove on in silence through the town. After crossing several rugged railroad tracks, Mr. Jesup turned off the main highway and pulled into a gas station located about twenty yards down a dirt road.

"You want something to drink?" asked Mr. Jesup.

"No, thank you. I'm not thirsty."

Mr. Jesup, while wiping the sweat off his brow, looked at John.

"Not thirsty."

"No, sir."

"Okay, son."

A train whistle was heard in the distance.

Mr. Jesup got out of the car to fill the tank up with gas. A black man came out of the convenience store whistling. He looked to be about the same age as Mr. Jesup. They shook hands and began talking. John was entranced by the man's green eyes.

"Maybe I should ask for something to drink. Maybe they have Orange Crush," thought a bored John, looking at the store.

John was reaching for the door handle when the stranger suddenly exclaimed, "Necessity's son is a hard thing, yes sir, a hard thing! Go right ahead and just pull up over yonder," he said pointing his finger toward an open field.

Mr. Jesup got back into the car. He drove over to the edge of the field. He turned the car off.

"Let's stretch our legs," he said.

"Yes, sir."

John followed Mr. Jesup into the field. They walked for a few minutes before stopping. Mr. Jesup gazed off into the distance.

"Beyond those trees there is Savannah River," Mr. Jesup intoned. "We'll be crossin' over her directly, crossin' over her right into the heart of Georgia."

John looked at the trees—mighty, white oaks lined up in a row.

"I'm gonna work hard, gonna work really hard, to get you to Florida, like I told your mother," said Mr. Jesup. "I need for you to do what I say."

"Yes, sir."

"There may be times it may not be easy. I hope not. But there may be those times, so you're gonna have to listen and do what I say."

"Yes, sir."

"I know you miss your mother. It's a terrible thing your father gone missin' and no one knows whether he is dead or alive. But they are not with us right now. For the next little while you are going to have to put all that aside. Oh, you're gonna think about them and their spirits are goin' to be here. That's only natural. It's so natural I don't think anyone can really ade-quat-ly explain why it is. All I know is you're goin' to have to travel beyond that. And I think deep down they would want that, too."

John was silent.

"I've been asked to do something. I am going to do it right because I thought it was right to do so. We don't know about tomorrow. Heck, we don't know about the next couple of hours. But we're here. We need to proceed. You understand what I am sayin'?"

"Yes, sir…kinda."

"Kinda?"

"Yes, sir."

Mr. Jesup smiled and said, "Now, you changed your mind about somethin' to drink?"

"You think they have any Orange Crush?"

"Like the bridegroom comin' from his pavilion, the champion runnin' his course," intoned Mr. Jesup. All the windows of Missy were down, and the morning spring air was rushing in every direction.

"Sir?" asked John, chugging his soda from the dark brown bottle.

"Look at the beauty, John—the clapping of all the hands!"

They crossed into Georgia. Missy was carrying them through fields of corn interspersed with peach orchards. White oaks still held court, although tall pines were coming into sight with ever increasing frequency. Through the branches, the sun was rising and shimmering with its rosy fingers through the topmost limbs of the oaks and pines, creating a carpet of dappled design beneath the trees. The sky was a heartbreaking azure blue; not a whisper of a cloud could be seen.

"New moon is afoot," said Mr. Jesup.

"Where?" asked John, looking out the window.

"Don't know exactly where, but it's out there looking down on us as we speak."

And as the car meandered through the rolling hills, riding on the crest of subtle waves of land on this back road known as the woodpecker trail, scenes of diverse Arcadian splendors delighted the soul. This was the Georgia Mr. Jesup loved. Its earth, its fruits, its skies, its tendency toward warmth and occasional blasts of chilled winds. Its human occupants were of a more mixed blessing and curse.

"Hungry?" asked Mr. Jesup.

"Yes, sir."

"We're approaching Zion. I know a place we can stop and eat. To tell you the truth, I know the place of Zion like the back of my hand."

"Did you grow up there?"

"In certain ways I did."

The truck sputtered on. Missy traveled the final bend of the road, drifting through ever-increasing visible signs of a town community. Houses stood either right next to the road or way off from the road in the middle of a cleared field.

"Look!" said John pointing his finger.

"What's that?" asked Mr. Jesup.

"Their yard has no grass. It's all dirt."

"Yeah, and looks pretty clean, too, don't it?"

"I guess so."

They passed the town sign of "Zion."

"Look at all the cars up ahead," said John.

"I see."

Mr. Jesup slowed Missy down considerably as they approached. While negotiating among the cars and trucks that jutted out into the roads, Mr. Jesup and John peered through the parked vehicles trying to discover what was happening.

"It must be a funeral. Somebody must have passed," said Mr. Jesup.

"There's a church. I can hear them singing inside."

"Yeah, that's Zion AME Church. I'm going to pull up here and see who is being buried."

John looked at the church. It was a long, rectangular, white-boarded structure. There was a tin roof that extended from the main building at the front entrance. Two thin posts held the roof up on both ends. A sign that read "Zion AME Church" hung over the front entrance. It looked as though the building might have been a gas station and general store in the past because where the gas pumps were located there was a long, rectangular slab of concrete with pots of flowers adorning its surface.

Crowds of people were standing in the doorway.

"You stay right here, John. I am going to check this out."

"Yes, sir."

John watched Mr. Jesup walk toward the church. One of the elderly ladies saw Mr. Jesup. She let out a scream and ran toward him with her arms wide open.

"I wonder if that is his mother," thought John.

The rest of the group from the front porch followed. Handshakes and hugs abounded, welcoming Mr. Jesup. Some of the folks pulled handkerchiefs out of their pockets to wipe away tears. Then everyone grew silent. A hush descended. John could hear a still, bass voice speaking but could not make out what was being said. Some of the people looked to the sky, others to the ground. Suddenly from inside the building came mournful wails and screams. Not one person in the groups standing outside flinched as the still, base voice continued to speak. There followed more sorrowful screams.

John looked straight out the window. Off to one side were a group of rose of Sharon bushes with lavender blooms. A red cardinal was fluttering around as though lost. The brown cardinal was nowhere to be seen.

"I hope you're not hurt," whispered John.

He looked for a nest but could not find one. He wondered what his mother was doing this very minute. He wished he were home. There was a sudden tapping on the driver's side window. John jumped. It was Mr. Jesup.

"John," said Mr. Jesup as he opened the driver's door. "Come on, we won't be too long. But we have to go; we have to go inside the church. Just stand next to me. We can't head south yet. Everything will be all right. Everything will be all right in the end."

John got out of the car. He walked close by Mr. Jesup's side, brushing against his clothing. Missy was still.

Several of the ladies and gentlemen approached them. The women wore huge, colorful hats. One was lavender, the others yellow, pink, blue. It reminded John of the rainbows he would occasionally see among stormy clouds. As they walked toward the entrance, the crowds parted to let Mr. Jesup and John through. Weeping, sighs of grief, the swishing of funeral home fans were the singular silent sounds among those gathered.

"Lord have mercy!" rang out the voice of the reverend as Mr. Jesup and John entered the sanctuary.

"Christ have mercy," responded the congregation.

"Lord...oh Lord have mercy!" proclaimed the Rev. Walden once again.

"Amen" resounded throughout at different intervals.

As they walked down the aisle, John looked neither to the left nor to the right of him, but straight ahead. The Rev. Horace Walden, standing behind the pulpit with a choir behind him in white robes and scarlet sashes around their necks, was what John focused on. As they walked closer to the front, there the open casket lay on ground level in front of the Rev. Walden. John noticed the contours of the body's face climbing beyond the borders of the casket. Its eyes were closed, and there was a faint smile visible from the side view.

"Right here, John," whispered Mr. Jesup as they entered the pew located several feet from the front. They sat. The choir started swaying back and forth. The organ swelled with full regalia of sound. Shouts were heard. The choir, clapping in rhythm, broke into song. A low, humming, deep, and melodious chorus rose up from the ground and ascended to the ceiling and beyond. Then from the group, a contralto stepped forward, her face joining the sounds above, with her body tremulous, shouting out words of grief and praise accompanying the song the choir had begun. Shouts of approval and recognition of said souls to the message sung reverberated from the congregation. John looked through the people in front of him to see a lady on the front pew shaking as well with both hands over her face. Suddenly, both her arms with clenched fists joined those gathered in the air above.

John, in spirit, went with everyone, entranced with the surrounding worship. He started to weep silently. He wondered whether his father was here, as well, right above the outstretched hands. He looked back at the coffin, seeing only one side. He wondered whether his father was laid there, as well. No sounds of recognition, only the feeling of his presence permeating the air around.

The singing and shouting went on. But for John, there was no time—no recognition of a sun drifting slowly toward the horizon.

Presently the Rev. Walden started preaching. John did not understand the greater import of what was said. He did catch in his mind phrases, words that he did not fully understand because he had not studied them in school. "The mustard seed of freedom to live and be" and "rights endowed equally to all by their Creator" and "the crosses every man, woman, and child carries with God's help, even those who are shot down."

Mr. Jesup on occasion would shout "Amen" with his hands clasped.

John was living in moments that would never leave him. Moments he would return to again and again. Moments that would offer new insights as his life traveled on. A singular trajectory unveiled itself before him, torn from top to bottom—a path that would identify him with people on the fringes of society—the other. Here he was among other others. He would be an example of the other. And like the outpouring of grief he sat among this day, he, too, would revisit similar scenes if not outwardly, then inwardly. And yet…and yet…as the service was drawn to its conclusion, there was present a still, small voice of hope amid the chaos. An unintended consequence that in some small way would bring relief and comfort, if only knowing that footprints were being left in the sand for others down the road to look on and console themselves with, that such a life had been lived.

But the anger, the anger mixed with despair and heartache. How does one walk humbly against such adversities? How can one act justly, justly…justly? How does one show mercy when none has been shown in return? Perhaps…perhaps only in the living, only in individual lives living among others, and the others can such questions only begin to be feebly answered, requiring a focus, a sharp focus concentrated on footprints in the far too often shifting sands. Such thoughts visited John later when reflecting on Zion and wondering about seminary as well.

"Here, Mr. Jesup, some sandwiches, chicken for the road, and a jug of iced sweet tea."

"Thanks, Mattie."

"I hear you are heading to Florida land?" asked Mattie.

"Yeah, going down the woodpecker trail. Keeping to the back roads as much as possible. I've got this boy to deliver to his aunt. John, this is Mattie."

"Pleased to meet you, John," said Mattie.

"Yes ma'am, me, too."

"New minister?" asked Mr. Jesup.

"New in town, fresh out of seminary. Right now, he's like a new broom. We're giving him several months to get broken in."

"Hope he can hang on without being thrown from the saddle."

"I do, too. I like the boy. He respects the elders. I don't see any evidence of him trying to lead us to the pastures. He's young enough to be my grandson, which is sobering to think about."

"He's got fire in his sermons on Sunday morning?"

"Enough to get by."

"Married?"

"No, but me and the sisters will keep an eye on him. Make sure… you know…nothing…," responded Mattie, looking at John.

Mr. Jesup responded laughing, "Yes, I do know…Ah, Rev. Walden!"

Mattie turned and said, "Rev. Walden, this is Jeremiah Jesup. Jeremiah, Rev. Horace Walden. And the reverend has told us that calling him just Horace would be just fine."

"Pleased to meet you, sir," responded the reverend.

"Likewise."

"Jeremiah grew up here. This is his home stomping grounds," said Mattie.

"Yes, baptized over the way in the creek. Come through on occasion. I am delivering this boy here, John, to his aunt in Florida."

"I see," said the Rev. Walden.

Mr. Jesup took the Rev. Walden by the arm and walked back toward the church. Mattie walked to John and exclaimed, "What grade are you in, John?"

Then Mr. Jesup proceeded with a further explanation to the reverend. "The boy's father has gone missing in Vietnam. I gardened for the family. So his mother is sending him to her sister. I think she plans to sell the house and move down herself. She just needed the boy to be out from under foot."

"Be careful. Mr. Jesup, there's a body laid out in the church because of a man trying to do a good deed."

"I know. She gave me a letter of explanation, just in case."

"Still."

"I know. We're traveling the back roads. May head over to the coast. It seems it may be easier on us closer to the ocean. Funny how that great body of water can soothe the most hateful. I just wanted to come through and check on how things were going. Not too good, I see."

"No, I am afraid this may be the opening salvo in an intense struggle coming up."

"This is a good church, with good people. You shepherd them as you would want to be, and they will hold your arms up in the battles—just like they did for Moses."

"Yes, sir."

"Just out of seminary, I understand."

"Yes, sir."

"Let me ask you. What do you think, what do you feel, reverend? Where will you shoulder the cross?"

"I don't follow."

"The pulpit or the streets?" asked Mr. Jesup.

"Well, the pulpit…"

"And the streets?"

"I don't know. I don't have a clear sense of calling in that direction."

"Anytime the Word is preached, we have to trust that it will bring beneficial results—even if we never see the ends."

"And…"

"And also remember, and I remind myself of this constantly: Jesus didn't hang around the local synagogue all the time."

"Yes, sir."

"The seeds of this town, this church was built on bloodshed, from the get-go. But look around and see all that is standing today. Whispers of hope. I will pray for you that you will act in the way it is shown to you by God."

"Thank you, sir."

Mr. Jesup placed his hand on the Rev. Walden's shoulder. They both looked to the ground. After a few moments, the Rev. Walden said, "Ashes to ashes, dust to dust."

"Plowed like a field, a heap of rubble...," said Mr. Jesup.

"A mound overgrown with thickets," finished the Rev. Walden.

Mr. Jesup continued, "There will be a war. Are you ready?"

"I don't see where I have any choice."

"You have a choice."

"I do, but I know that warming myself by the fire, living with the silence, will drown me."

"You may end up like the man in the church building."

"I may. But I would have been faithful to my vows."

"That's true, and we know what happens on the third day, anyway, right?"

"Yes, sir. We do."

"One more question and then I need to get John on down to Florida."

"What is that?"

"You alone?"

"You mean is there another person in my life beyond the church walls?"

"I do."

"I have not pursued that. I feel like, for me, it would distract me from my calling."

"Yes, that could happen, as well as being distracted by not having someone. It is in the matter of choosing...choosing wisely. But I would venture to say all of us need a shoulder from somewhere."

"Loneliness is a heavy burden at times, I will admit."

"Yes, and that shoulder, whoever that person may be, make sure it is a shoulder you can...how can I put this...love and embrace regardless of what anyone else says or thinks. And that includes Mattie."

The Rev. Walden smiled and said, "For me, I feel like it is a tall order."

"Well, if you haven't experienced it already, there's a reason Cupid has an arrow and wings."

"I believe in that, sir."

"Remember…whoever…whoever that person may be…just so long as they are flesh and blood. In my book, that's the only requirement."

For a moment, a rising ruddy coloring spread over the Rev. Walden's face. It looked as though he wanted to speak but couldn't. He wished he could but couldn't. He was dumbstruck. Instead, he took his fist and pounded it in the palm of the other hand several times.

Mr. Jesup laid his hands on the Rev. Walden's head and whispered, "You are a blessing, my brother."

"Jeremiah! Jeremiah! Are y'all planning to spend the night?" yelled Mattie.

Deus Ex Machina

The Wayfaring Strangers
The Hematite Girl
Tattooed Tom
Madame Estella

In silence, Mr. Jesup and John drove away from Zion toward the coast. Eating chicken wings and pimento cheese sandwiches and drinking the sweet tea out of mason jars, both observed the dignity of what transpired earlier in their own way, as the mid-afternoon beams of the sun guided them through the shadows of the tall pines covering the road ahead. They crossed into the southern portion of Georgia. Missy was carrying them through orchards of stunted peach trees, interspersed with tall pines reaching higher and higher into the blue sky. Off in the distance, cypress trees with Spanish moss hanging from their limbs were coming into sight with ever-increasing frequency. As the sun made its journey behind the travelers, its rosy hue reflected off the pines and cypresses, glistening in the limbs and foliage into a spangled array of different intensities of light. Ahead, the sky was vast and vacant. Then suddenly, John spotted the thinned fringe of a fingernail held to a candle just above the horizon through the trees. The new moon was coming out of its shell. He was comforted, but this time in a way different from how he was before.

"Not too far to the coast. I know a place where we can put up for the night," said Mr. Jesup. He began humming the tune "The Wayfaring Stranger."

Missy alighted among slight hills, riding the crest of subtle waves of land that opened into vast, flat surfaces. The environs spoke of a diverse, mysterious landscape that haunted the soul. This was an area Mr. Jesup always treated with the greatest respect with a certain hopeful yet wary eye. They were truly alone in fields that were not only alive and teeming during the day, but much animated during the nights.

Suddenly, there was a loud bang.

The startled Mr. Jesup looked out the rearview mirror. John looked at Mr. Jesup.

"Oh, not now…not now, sweet Missy," muttered Mr. Jesup.

He pulled Missy over and got out of the car. He walked to the rear. John heard him kick one of the tires and let out a low whistle.

John sat still, looking out over the horizon through the windshield. The fields were flat and expansive. A silvery, watery mirage glimmered off in the distance. From the far edge of the field, tall cypress trees with accompanying Spanish moss were much larger and majestic than seen first from afar. They were much closer to the road, suggesting a wild expanse beyond. To John's right was a forest housing the last remnants of the mighty white and red oaks. The rolling hills had long since vanished. And ahead was the road they were traveling on. It stretched out in a linear fashion seemingly into eternity. Mr. Jesup told John they were on a secondary road, a road less traveled. Indeed, they had only passed one or two cars over the previous hour.

"John, come back here!" shouted Mr. Jesup.

"Yes, sir," shouted John as he scrambled out of Missy.

"We've got a flat. Picked up a nail. And I'm sorry to say my spare is as flat as well. Forgot to take care of the situation. You know, being in the city lulled me to sleep in that matter."

Mr. Jesup looked down the road, and then across the field. He scratched his head.

"If my memory serves me correctly, we're about halfway through a lonely stretch of road."

The sun glistened through the trunks of the cypress trees. A few finger-like clouds were forming as the sky turned from blue bleeding into a rosy color. There was a rustling sound from the forest. Mr. Jesup and John peered into the cypress trees but could not see anything. Then from among the branches of a cluster of low-lying bushes a hematite hand appeared. Then a second hematite hand appeared. For a moment, the hands seemed suspended in mid-air, detached. Then slowly the hands moved in sync parting the branches to reveal a hematite face.

It was an oval-shaped face. Its Oriental eyes peered at Mr. Jesup and John. The black hair was braided and gathered in a circular fashion on top of the head. The lips were thin, with a slight smile. The chin extended out. It was a still face, with a wistful, glowing countenance.

"Hey there!" shouted Mr. Jesup.

Instinctively, one of the fingers from the hematite hand covered the lips indicating to keep silent. Then the hematite person stepped out of the bushes into the open. It appeared to be a young girl.

She wore a brown, plaid dress with a piece of twine around the waist, tattered white socks, and holey tennis shoes that had seen better days. Draped around her left shoulder was a leather strap with a water canteen and machete attached. She sprinted to Mr. Jesup and John, leaping over the undergrowth that separated them. In a flash, she was by their side. She smiled. Her teeth were pristine white and all accounted for.

"You live around here?" asked Mr. Jesup.

She nodded her head "yes." She pointed behind her.

"What's the matter, cat got your tongue?"

Her face grew still. She frowned and shook her head slowly. Her thin lips parted. A low, imperceptible sound came from her throat. Her hands began moving rapidly and started hitting against each other as if trying to give out a signal.

"Oh, Lord, you can't talk. Please forgive me. I didn't know," said Mr. Jesup.

She nodded her head. She smiled and took Mr. Jesup's hand. She extended the water canteen to him.

"Thank you. Here, John, have some water," said Mr. Jesup.

John took the canteen and began to drink. The water was cool and refreshing. It streamed down the sides of his mouth.

"Thank you," he said while handing the canteen back to Mr. Jesup. He took a few swigs and then handed it back to the girl.

"We have a flat tire. And I've no spare," Mr. Jesup motioned to the girl.

The girl alighted over to look closer at the tire. Her hands felt around its circumference. Her hands stopped. They found something among the ridges of the tire. She toyed with the area for a few moments. She looked at the tire, gently caressing its surface, all the while making a low guttural sound from her throat. She stood. In her left hand was a long, silver nail.

"I bet we picked that up at Zion," muttered Mr. Jesup. He gestured once more indicating that there was no spare. "Is there anyone who could help us?"

The girl nodded her head "yes." She tilted her head, listening. Suddenly she looked off in the direction from where she came. She dropped the silver nail. Her eyes were frozen in terror. Mr. Jesup and John looked in the same direction. Off in the distance, a cloud of dust was seen ascending into the air among the tall cypress trees. She motioned to Mr. Jesup not to say a word about her. She ducked down and sprinted off in the opposite direction across to a mighty oak situated about fifty yards from Missy. She disappeared to the other side of the oak. John picked up the silver nail from the ground.

Mr. Jesup and John stood in silence as the dust came closer to them. It appeared that it was a four-wheel drive vehicle bouncing among the ditches in the field.

Mr. Jesup drew John close to his side.

"Not a word about that girl," he told John.

"Yes, sir."

The cloud of dust billowed with withering intensity as it came closer. The creaking and clanging of the four-wheel drive vehicle grew louder and louder. It spurted out onto the secondary highway. As its driver turned toward Mr. Jesup and John, the wheels squealed against the gravely, asphalt pavement. Then it squealed to a halt. The dust evaporated into the air, as the man jumped out of the vehicle.

"Having trouble?" he yelled. The man's eyes were luminous, good-natured, casting the merriment of their aqua blue color toward the pair, although possessing a kind of animal ferocity. He was tall and wore a sleeveless shirt that revealed his muscular arms decorated with an assortment of tattoos, one resembling a parrot. John recognized the bird. He had seen a real one in a National Geographic magazine. There was a crimson scarf fluttering around his neck in the breeze. He sported dark, curly hair that covered his ears where one golden earring decorously dangled. He wore a thick, dark moustache. His hat was broad-brimmed, woven with palm-leaf. His scimitar ran almost the length of his legs, and a rifle was hoisted over one shoulder.

John was transfixed. It was as if he had stumbled onto a character from a high seas adventure story. There were warm stirrings in John that he did not understand, especially in his torso.

Mr. Jesup was immutable, cautious, and would weigh his words. He took John's hand and squeezed it.

"Have a flat. Picked up a nail," said Mr. Jesup leaning over to pick up the silver nail. He raised it into the air.

"Too bad," replied the man.

"And we don't have a spare," continued Mr. Jesup.

"That's really bad. Seems you have got a shortage of luck today." The man scrutinized Mr. Jesup and John and asked, "Your boy?"

"He is my ward, my employer's son. I have a letter from his mother verifying our trip. I am delivering him to his aunt in Florida."

"I believe you. Seems you should be heading south rather than east. You are almost at the Atlantic's edge."

"I know, I grew up in the Zion area not far from here. I wanted to stay off the main road and drive down the coast. Felt things would work better that way."

"Yes, I understand what you are saying. Plenty of hiding places along the coast."

The man walked over to the tire and studied it. He took his rifle and with its barrel skirted the surface next to the whitewalls.

"I'm thinking a plug might do the trick. Might hold off long enough to deliver your ward."

"That's encouraging," responded Mr. Jesup.

"The nearest gas station is quite a distance from here. And as you know, not much traffic in this area. The cars and trucks that do pass through are not inclined to stop for strangers…like you two. And if they did, I would be mighty suspicious of their intentions."

"I see."

"Why don't you hop in my truck, and we'll go back to my boss's plantation and see what we've got. We might can swap out the tires. The boy can sit by me and ride shotgun."

"We don't mind waiting here."

"It will be dark soon, and if something happened to you two, I wouldn't want it on my conscience. Besides, we may not have anything to help you out with, and you might end up having to wait until morning. You've got extra clothes?"

"We have a few things."

"Well, get them, and let's get going. Oh, by the way, you might want to lock up your car. No telling who might be lurking about."

The man headed toward his four-wheeler, while Mr. Jesup retrieved their suitcases.

"Come on, John. We will be all right. Just don't talk too much," said Mr. Jesup.

Mr. Jesup locked the car but then quickly unlocked it. He patted Missy's hood.

"You ride shotgun," the man pointed to John, patted the passenger seat, and smiled, opening the door so they could climb into the four-wheel truck.

The stranger started the vehicle. Mr. Jesup was about to introduce himself and John to the man, but with the buoyance and noise of the four-wheeler it would have taken too much effort.

As they drove down the road toward the grove of cypress trees, Mr. Jesup noticed the man occasionally looking around, as if expecting someone or something. Mr. Jesup looked back at Missy, forlorn and deserted in no telling what kind of country and began wondering if he would ever see her again.

Suddenly, they turned onto a dirt road. It was rough because of the occasional dips caused by erosion. Pebbles were scattered throughout the drive, the sand soft. In a rainstorm, this passageway would prove treacherous. Mr. Jesup made one parting glance at Missy to see if anyone had come to her rescue. The area was vacant. He tried to look over to the tree where the girl had hidden. But they were traveling too fast for a close inspection.

As the road twisted and turned, it became narrower, with the cypress trees advancing closer to road's edge, until eventually huge limbs traversed over the road with huge clumps of Spanish moss dangling in the air. The sun was intermittently shooting forth its rays as it descended closer to the horizon. A dark rose sheen was beginning to saunter forth over the Atlantic. Mr. Jesup looked up into the Southern heavens. He spotted Venus sparkling and glittering, wishing he were driving in her direction. He wondered if Mars lurked nearby.

As the car bounced over a deep ravine, they passed an intricate, multi-wired fence and open gate. The forest was thick and dark. John looked over to his right and noticed the land was transmuting itself into a swamp.

The man saw John looking out and shouted, "The alligators are still lingering around, and there are panthers about. So it pays not to wander too far in the dark, even on the road!"

John remembered stories about the Swamp Fox and his adventures. He wondered if the driver of the four-wheeler was anything like that man. "So, this is the kind of place he hung out," John thought, scanning the terrain in greater detail. He was not quite sure that hearing about such things was more exciting than the reality of the situation.

They turned a sharp corner, and suddenly in full view was a white, two-story mansion with several large angel oaks gracing its perimeters. The front center of the mansion possessed an oval design. Ionic columns supported the front portal's roof. Over the front entrance was a balcony with ornate posts. There were tall windows encased with intricate moldings. Four or five lengthy steps led to the front porch. Boxwoods were planted bordering the mansion.

The vehicle stopped.

The driver sat still for a moment looking around. Mr. Jesup and John dared not say a word. The man turned to Mr. Jesup, grinned, and said, "Welcome to my mistress's little abode."

"Some shack," thought Mr. Jesup.

"Sherman missed this place, so here it stands."

Unseen hounds were heard baying and barking from a nearby barn. Their howls rung with a hideous peal as everyone got out of the vehicle.

From the front entrance, an elderly woman wrapped in a mink stole stepped out. Her black walking cane was held by a bony, pale white hand wearing several rings that glistened in the last of the sun's rays for the day. She wore a green dress that almost extended to the ground with a matching hat. Her hair was gray. She wore sunglasses. The lines in her face were etched deep. As she approached the arriving party with the black cane scraping the ground, John noticed an abundance of facial powder, the dark lines over her eyebrows, and her dark red lips. The lipstick wavered over the lips proper. A bloodless contentious expression from her face shined. She smiled, but it was of a kind that repelled rather than encouraged a similar response from others.

"My boss lady," said the man in a whisper.

"Welcome, boys, to my plantation," she announced.

"I am sorry, ma'am, for the intrusion, but we picked up a nail somewhere along the way, and have a flat, and no spare on top of all that. Your man was very gracious to try to help us out so we can be on our way," said Mr. Jesup.

"I wouldn't suggest nighttime travel around in these parts," said the boss lady. "But as you can see," she pointed her cane back toward the mansion, "I believe we have a spare room or two that can accommodate you for the evening. My boy here sleeps in the barn with the other animals."

"Yes ma'am, and we are grateful for your hospitality."

"Good gracious, what are Southerners if not hospitable? Tom, why don't you go run and see if we have a tire that will do the trick. Take the little tyke with you. He looks like the adventurous type to me. Your name, son?"

"John."

"Welcome, John. Now run along and don't let my boy be a bad influence on you." She smirked and then laughed.

John looked at Mr. Jesup.

"It is okay, run along like the lady…suggested," Mr. Jesup said.

"Come on, son," said Tom.

John and Tom walked toward the barn. John was relieved to leave the elderly woman's gaze. But he felt for Mr. Jesup and hoped he would be all right.

John took two steps for every one of Tom's. On occasion, he would look up at Tom's muscular arms and shoulders. The tattoo parrot was on the side that John could see and seemed to be winking at him as Tom's arms swung back and forth. He wanted to pet the parrot to see how it felt running his fingers along its feathered body. Tom saw John looking and laughed.

He said, "When we get to the barn, little Johnnie, I'll introduce you to my best friend, Patience."

"Come in…I'm sorry, I didn't catch your name?"

"I haven't said, but it is Jeremiah Jesup. And yours?"

"Madame Estella."

They approached the double front doors. On both sides of the entrance were two large fern plants potted in ornate, gargantuan white vases. There was a beige side table to one side whose surface was thinly splattered with bird droppings. Stained glass windows encased both sides of the doors. Hues of various shades of brown and green glass entwined with metal strips gave the windows a tangled, murky view of what lay beyond. And as they entered through the doors, the hounds continued to bark and howl off in the distance.

After entering the mansion, Madame Estella suddenly said, "Now turn around and look at the stain windows with the lowering sun shining through."

"What a beautiful floral design," exclaimed Mr. Jesup. "You could not tell from the outside."

"My favorite time of the day," said the boss lady.

"I am a gardener by trade."

"So you are especially appreciative."

"Yes, ma'am."

"They're rumored to be Tiffany's. I have no papers to confirm that."

"They are beautiful regardless."

"You can make out the flowers even at night. They possess a certain potency."

"Have you lived here long?" asked Mr. Jesup.

"All my life, never have known anything else."

"What keeps this place going?"

"Oh…all kind of things. This hallway is always too dark. Let's go into the front parlor room."

When entering the room, Madame Estella made a repeated stabbing of the black cane into the thick oriental rugs.

"Have a seat," she commanded.

⁂

As Tom and John entered the barn, there was an explosive snorting and vociferous sounds of distress and anger from one of the horse stalls.

"Patience! Patience!" yelled Tom. "Patience! We've got company!"

Tom walked toward the stall. John stood frozen at the entrance, not knowing whether to run back toward the house and Mr. Jesup or not.

The horse was a black stallion of huge dimensions. As Tom approached, the horse began to settle down.

"Patience, is this any way to act? What are people going to think, especially our guests?"

The loud snorts slowly turned into a neighing of a quiet disposition.

"Come here, Johnnie boy!"

John questioned the wisdom of such a move.

Tom turned toward John and with a mocking, high pitched tone of voice said, "He's not going to hurt you. He knows what I'll do to him if he so does. He sees you are with me. Besides, I have some sugar cubes I will let you feed him with. He likes sugar cubes. It really calms the beast in him. Come on."

John walked slowly toward Tom. All the sounds in the barn became still. It seemed all the planks, all the wasps, all the pieces of straw were holding their collective breaths.

Tom clutched John's left wrist.

"It seems there are two animals I need to calm down. Here," he said, smiling.

Tom turned John's left hand upward and dropped several sugar cubes into it. Tom held one cube back and held it in front of John's face.

"Care for one?" he asked John.

John opened his mouth.

"See how sweet it is? Explains why Patience gets so submissive. Now go on. Feed Patience."

John slowly walked toward the stall half-door. But instead of holding his hand out, he placed the sugar cubes one at a time, in a row on the flat top surface of the stall. Patience immediately licked up each cube with a loud slurping of his tongue. John jumped back.

"Here, take this brush and comb his mane while I go look for a tire."

John took the brush, looking at Tom's tattooed parrot on his shoulder.

"You like Long John?" asked Tom.

"Who is he?"

Tom pointed to his arm.

"I do," responded John. "I wish he were alive so I could pet him."

Tom let out a loud laugh and said, "Boy he is alive. You just have to know which tune to whistle."

"I don't know how to whistle."

"You will…oh you will in a few years, Johnnie boy, you will. Brush, and I'll be back soon."

John felt faint. Tom walked away whistling.

Madame Estella had a servant serve tea and scones.

"Getting nigh 4 p.m. Teatime!"

Mr. Jesup noticed that the servant bore a faint resemblance to the girl they had encountered out in the fields after their flat. He wondered if that girl had run away or was playing hooky.

While sipping tea, Mr. Jesup tried to restrain his eating, for he and John had not had a decent repast that day.

"You must be hungry! Eat up. There's more where that came from."

After a while, the late afternoon sun's rays lazily glided over the furniture, anticipating the coming of night. Estella sat wearing sunglasses. The conversation became stilted and drowsy. The shadows were creeping around hidden corners of the room and furniture, foreshadowing deeper shadows to come. Estella's head began to droop, the sunglasses slowly inching down her nose. Mr. Jesup felt as if he were in an art museum where pieces were strategically placed for appreciative viewing, including the living model seated before him. He felt a chill and shuddered. It seemed the winds in the room were wooing the frozen bosom of the North. Suddenly there was the stamping of feet out on the front porch—heavy stomps back and forth mixed in with lighter-weighted ones. The winds, being angered, puffed away, turning to the dew-dropping South.

Estella stirred and murmured, "What's that?"

"I believe our little men are back," responded Mr. Jesup.

The front doors flew open, and afterward Tom and John entered the room.

"I'm sorry, sir, we have no tire to fit your car. We'll have to head out in the morning to the nearest gas station and see if they have one. It's a good twenty miles from here."

"Well…" Mr. Jesup was wondering what to say.

"And of course, you two will spend the night," said Madame Estella. "We have a guest room down the hallway with a couple of beds."

"We hate to be trouble and intrude on your kindness," said Mr. Jesup.

"Fiddlesticks! You are no trouble. Now, son, I know you're thirsty. How about a soda before supper?"

"I'm okay."

"No you're not. I can tell by looking at you."

"Do you have an Orange Crush?"

Madame Estella laughed, "I'll be right back." She took off her mink-collared coat and walked back into the dark hallway.

Over in the far corner, John noticed a grand piano with a vase of purple hydrangeas sitting on its surface. Tom noticed the direction of John's eyes.

"You play?" Tom asked.

"Yes, sir, a little."

"You need to tickle these ivories. I know the boss lady will appreciate it. Those keys have been awfully lonesome. Could do with a little touch of human flesh."

John was not a happy camper with that suggestion.

"Come on over," Tom walked to the piano and sat in a Victorian settee with crimson velvet upholstery next to the instrument. He crossed his legs and began cracking his knuckles. "I'll be the percussion section, and perhaps old Long John here will whistle in harmony," he said smiling. After a few moments he then said, "We're waiting."

John looked at Mr. Jesup.

"Go on, John; we need to be mindful of how they are taking care of us in our predicament."

John was forced to face the predicament he was in. He walked to the piano and sat down. He could smell Tom, the hay, the muck in the barn, and the black stallion. It was as if they were listening as well. He decided to play his first recital piece, "The Wigwam." Hearing hounds starting to bay again in the distance, away he went, and he repeated it several times because the piece was only a single page, hoping the lady with his soda would soon come.

"One large Orange Crush! I assumed you would like it chilled! Tom, be neighborly; why don't you walk Mr. Jesup around the place?"

"Those hounds never let up," muttered Tom as he and Mr. Jesup approached the barn doors. It was dark. The cicadas were singing in chorus.

"You been here long?" asked Mr. Jesup.

"All my life; never have known anything else."

"Have you been to school?"

Tom stopped. "Look around. This place, this earth, those woods, those swamps, those fields, the animals—they have been my teachers. I am their star pupil. I am what you might call the teacher's pet."

"You seem to express yourself well."

"There is the library up at the house. I guess those books have something to do with that, particularly that Shakespeare. He's also helped me figure people out."

"Does the madam treat you right?"

"Yeah, sort of; she's full of charms—an actress who is always looking for the lights."

The barn door grinded against the graveled ground as Tom pushed the huge, wooden door to one side. The inside was as black as the night.

"Stay here," said Tom. He walked into the darkness.

Mr. Jesup stood at the entrance smelling fresh cut hay. He could hear Tom's footsteps off in the distance inside the barn. Mr. Jesup strained his eyes to follow where he went. But the figure disintegrated into the air like the mist of fox fires.

Mr. Jesup heard the creak of a door spirited through the air. He looked toward the night sky and saw the laboring fingernail moon ascend. Strangely, he felt comforted.

A door slammed. Mr. Jesup heard the whinnying of a horse. He instinctively walked to one side of the entrance. The slow trot of a horse beat against the hardened dirt floor. Then suddenly, from the abyss, emerged Tom astride the black stallion bareback, with a brown burlap sack over the horse's shoulders.

"This is Patience," said Tom.

"What an animal!"

Mr. Jesup noticed a flashlight flickering on and off in the distance.

"Now you have seen him. I need to ride around and check on a few things. If you want to go on back to the house, be my guest. I am sure Johnnie-boy would like to see you, particularly if the missus has not drifted off to sleep."

"Thank you."

Tom and Patience pranced in a circular pattern several times with a sly circumspection of the surrounding woods. Then Tom thrust his legs into the horse. They immediately galloped off into the fields in the direction of the outlying cypress trees. The flickering flashlight had disappeared.

Mr. Jesup looked again toward the night sky. There emanated a celestial brightness. A shooting star spirited across the evening canvas. A nightingale sang. And then he heard the snapping of a twig among the bushes located nearby.

"Who's there?" he whispered.

His eyes caught something among two branches, the appearance of two hematite hands with two ends of a twig held. The branches, drawing back, revealed the hematite oval face with slender eyes and braided circular black hair peering toward him. It was the same face he and John had seen earlier in the day on the secondary highway. Immediately, she drew her finger to her lips. Mr. Jesup did likewise. She glided through the bushes toward him. She stood still, bringing her clutched hands in front of her in midair. She made sure Mr. Jesup blocked her from the mansion. She furiously moved her hands up and down, up and down, while at the same time nodding her head in like manner. She mimicked picking up an item and placing it to one side.

"The tire is fixed?" asked Mr. Jesup.

She nodded yes. She walked several steps away from Mr. Jesup toward one side of the broad and beaten path between the mansion and the barn. She motioned for him to follow and repeated the gesture of her finger to her lips. Mr. Jesup did the same. As they approached the house, they heard the piano playing.

"Anything will do…," repeated Estella lounging on the crimson Victorian couch. "Anything will do, as long as it's quiet and nice-like. I've had a busy day and I'm very tired. So I'll dance with you in my head." She then lifted her gin and tonic in midair, thrusting it forward toward John and the piano.

John hesitated for a moment. He called up the alacrity of spirit from some unknown, previously unexplored quarter of him by lightly playing "Come, Dance with Me," a song from his red third grade John Thompson book he had been practicing and memorizing before leaving home. He played it through several times, feeling more secure hiding within the music. But after the fifth time, he stopped. He next played "Evening Prayer." With this piece, he went much more slowly than even the moderato suggested by the composer, partly because of faulty memory recall, but he wanted to do as little talking with Estella as possible. He thought of Tom. He wanted him to come into the room and laugh.

After the third time of playing the piece, he stopped. Anticipating a comment from the mistress of the mansion, he sat in silence. But nothing was said. There was a slight snoring sound. He slowly turned around. She was asleep. The gin and tonic glass was on a side table, empty. What should he do? He was afraid to start the piece again for fear of waking her. He was also afraid of getting off the stool for the same reason. So he sat still and looked out the window.

And then from the recesses of a magnolia tree next to the mansion, he saw two branches, one of which contained a bloom, drawing back revealing Mr. Jesup with a finger to his lips. He motioned for John to come outside. He then repeated the movement of his finger to his lips.

John was scared. His heart began beating faster and faster. His ears were throbbing with a pulsating loud noise. He was sure Estella would awaken at any moment. But she was not stirring. The musical tones of a heavier breathing ensued. A pattern emerged. A rhythm began. This gave John courage. He slowly turned his body on the piano bench toward the entrance hallway door. The stool did not creak. He was suddenly thankful for the thick carpets lying across the floor. When he first entered the room, he thought the carpets suffocating. Now they were liberating, assisting in his escape. He stood. He walked slowly, daring not to tiptoe for fear of some of his bones cracking like Tom's fingers. Hounds once more bayed in the distance. He stopped. She continued her song with deep breathing. He was only a few steps to the entrance into the dark hallway. He looked back at Estella. Beyond her was the large window that framed the huge magnolia tree with the bloom and Mr. Jesup facing John. Mr. Jesup's countenance was of great comfort and strength. Suddenly, Estella stirred. Her hand involuntarily tapped the black cane. It wavered. In an instant, it slid to the edge of the couch. But it was caught by the excessive baroque wood carvings along its borders.

John stood still for a few moments. Estella slipped back into heavy breathing. The patterns reemerged. John took two large steps into the dark hallway. Before him to the right was the front door. He tiptoed quickly to the entrance. He gently placed his hands on the knob. It slowly turned. At first, it seemed to have stuck. Then suddenly a latch clicked. The door came forward. He listened for any movement in the drawing room. Everything was still.

John opened the door only wide enough for him to slip through. Then slowly, carefully, he closed the door. He quickly walked from the front porch onto the grounds, where he saw Mr. Jesup in front of him with an extended hand.

"Come on, John," he whispered. "We need to make tracks."

The hematite girl was at the red dirt drive by the barn, motioning for them to follow.

"What about our suitcases?" asked John.

"Forget about them," responded Mr. Jesup.

And so, silently, under the silver gleam of moon's light, the trio set out, still keeping to one side of the road, lest someone came down the drive. At first, they walked at a fast pace. But the farther they were from the white mansion, the faster they went, breaking into a slow run. Through the tall cypress trees with hanging Spanish moss they ran. John felt safe with their presence because he felt they were assisting in hiding them from full view. He kept looking at the road ahead, straining to see Missy but also keeping an eye out for any wandering alligator or panther. Soon, they ran around the double wired entrance out into the open fields. As they topped a slight hill, they saw Missy off in the distance for the first time. John wanted to shout out, "There she is!" but kept quiet. He could hear the hounds no more. They ran faster. Closer and closer they came to Missy under the clouded majesty of the rising moon. The firmament glowed and spangled with a multitude of living sapphires, its field sowed with thousands upon thousands of gleaming stars and planets.

They sprinted out onto the secondary highway. Breathless, they arrived at Missy. Mr. Jesup immediately went to check the tire. Everything was repaired. She had plugged the hole and pumped air back into the tire. They were ready to leave.

"My child, oh my child, what we owe you is beyond anything we could ever pay with money," whispered Mr. Jesup hugging the girl. He reached for his wallet.

The hematite girl stopped him. She gleamed and smiled. She handed John a few pebbles. She then turned and darted into the woods.

"My Hesperus, oh my Hesperus that led the starry host rode brightest. Yes sir, she rode brightest. Come on, John, we got to get out of here right now!" They scrambled into Missy. The engine started, and off they traveled down the silver graveled secondary highway back toward Zion with neither daring to look but straight ahead.

Off among the cypress trees under the Spanish moss, a lone figure on a black stallion sat. He waved his hand, shedding a tear and whispered, "Love all, trust a few. Do wrong to none."

The Morning Star

Miss Jessie
The Party Line

After regrouping in Zion, the next morning at the Rev. Walden's apartment, Mr. Jesup and John continued to travel toward the heartland of Northern Florida, not directly along the coast but now about a hundred miles inland. The hills slumbered into a more rolling stance until the environs fanned out into flat surfaces all around. A hard, straight line separated earth from heaven. As the miles went by, the pines became taller and thinner. The cypress trees gathered in smaller clusters rather than spreading out. Along the secondary highway, the terrain succumbed to marshes, swamps, and dark water streams and tributaries that spread to the roads and on occasion skirted the tires of Missy. But then periodically the enriched vegetated waters drew back from the road, carrying Missy over on bridges. As the chariot of fire started its descent, they motored over the last bridge leading from Georgia into the Feast of Flowers. They had arrived. They had driven into the woods of the lakes.

Mr. Jesup started singing again from the hymn "A Wayfaring Stranger." Gum-sweet wood appeared. The road was much smoother. John could feel the midafternoon rays bathing and massaging his body. He let the warm elements break across his limbs, caressing his face and neck. He leaned his head back. He pretended sleep. He rested his hands on his thighs. On occasion, barely opening his eyes, he looked out over the windshield, glimpsing at the tall, hard palm trees coming toward him. He thought of Tom.

Mr. Jesup started singing more loudly. John opened his eyes and smiled contentedly.

"We gave them the slip! We gave them the slip, John!" exclaimed Mr. Jesup.

John laughed a bittersweet laugh.

"We sure did, Mr. Jesup."

"We've had us an adventure!"

"You reckon the Swamp Fox did the same thing?" asked John.

"Sure, only he did it every day for some time. You like the Swamp Fox?"

"I like to hear about him."

"I see. You hungry?"

"Yes, sir."

"There's a place down the road apiece we will stop at—along about sunset. It's a lady's house, a real lady's cracker shack, Miss Jessie's place."

"How do you know her?"

"She was an early teacher of mine. Before moving to Zion, my family lived where she lives. In fact, I was ushered into the world at that place. The woods and earth there are the portals of my existence."

"Really?"

"Really. She may have something for us to eat, but if not, I know of another place else we could go. But she will have something for us, I know. She always has something for anybody and everybody. And she has a phone, a party line. We need to call your mother, let her know we are alive and well. She's probably called your aunt and knows we have not arrived yet."

Mother—John had not thought of her since the beginning of their adventure on late afternoon the day before. That struck him as odd, different. He felt different. He could not put words to what he felt, but it was different. It was similar to the feeling he had when learning how to ride a bike. Only this time, the feeling meant something bigger, something profound; only he didn't know that word at the time. He felt a stirring inside him.

"Where is your mother?" asked John.

"My mother passed a long time ago. Even before Miss Jessie started teaching me. I grew up with my grandmother. She lived not far from Miss Jessie. But grandmother passed, too. Everybody I was ever related to directly by blood has passed. They all have passed."

"Even your father?"

"He, too. He went to war and never came back. We don't know where he finally laid his head down for that final rest."

John thought of his father. Mr. Jesup suddenly realized that thought as well. He patted John's left shoulder.

"I think you're going to like Miss Jessie. Although older, she's still fit. Nothing scares her except being scared. She came out years ago to live where we were living then. It was tough. It was a wilderness. Still is in many ways. But she walked through it. Her husband didn't. He left. Didn't last a year. Went back to the creature comforts. He begged. He pleaded. She didn't leave. Just waved goodbye. Only thing she wanted from him was the typewriter so she could write. Besides, she had her old, big, black mutt, a shotgun, a bottle of whiskey that never ran dry, and a tractor to keep her company. Then she started planting orange trees, selling oranges to people out at the side of the road. What more could she want?"

Missy was getting warm inside, so Mr. Jesup rolled his window down. John did the same.

"Smell the breeze. Smell the blossoms?" asked Mr. Jesup.

"Yes, sir, sure do."

"We are in Florida land." Mr. Jesup laughed.

John tingled all over.

"How many more miles to Miss Jessie's?" John asked.

"A few more hills and dales to pass through, a couple of rivers to go over, and we'll be there."

A gentle sleep swept over John. He curled himself against the back of his seat while looking out the passenger side window. The blue western sky was layered with finger-like flattened white cloud puff balls that extended across the span of hidden powdered stars. The wispy moon whose traces blended in with the clouds was slowly descending, becoming larger, more distinct. It would soon disappear, slowly enveloped and caressed by the gentle clouds.

Missy was swaying over the smooth road. Green, shady banks suddenly gave way to expanded vistas of yellow-rosy smooth lakes, spotted with blooming lily pads and gothic arching trees. Bushes with flying branches resembling buttresses of a cathedral circled around the bases of the giant oaks. And then just as suddenly, the scenery slipped back into thick forests and green, shady banks. Back and forth, back and forth, these scenes went. Green, shady banks then yellow-rosy smooth lakes, green, shady banks then yellow-rosy smooth lakes then back to shady banks, pulsating with a rhythm that complemented the movement of Missy, as it back and forth sped in linear fashion down the smooth road, and then took a turn to the left at a forty-five-degree angle down a white, sandy drive, under thick canopies of centennial trees.

A burst of brilliant light reflected into the passenger rearview mirror, thrusting into John's face, causing him to heave then relax.

"We're here! We've arrived at Miss Jessie's place!" shouted Mr. Jesup.

"Look, John! There she is!"

A rectangular shaped house stood among palm trees and bushes. It was light green and had a tin roof. A slightly slanted porch wrapped around the front, with simple, direct columns with no fancy frills on top. Off to one side was an extended open garage. An old model T was parked underneath. Chickens were pecking around the tires and the sides of the driveway. A rainbow-colored rooster stood off to one side surveying his harem. Surrounding the house were groves of orange trees. To one side was a vegetable garden with green beans and squash mixed together. Several rows of green corn stalks stood, suggesting a bountiful crop in the days ahead.

John was intrigued by plants sprouting large, purple oblong vegetables or fruit. He had never seen such plants. And on the other side of the house was a barn that looked at least a hundred years old. Its tin roof was of a rusty, burnt orange color. It sloped dramatically at an acute angle from its apex. The walls were made of old boards of varying sizes and shaped with spaces between vaguely exposing bundles of hay, stacked in the side stalls. A tractor was parked in the wide, interior section that extended the whole length of the barn. Its huge, black tires were caked with dried mud. Brooms, shovels, anvils, rakes, and old license plates from bygone years graced the open, interior walls. Two mules could be seen extending their heads from the corrals, looking to see who just drove up.

As the sun sparkled among the scenery, dew droplets from a recent shower glittered, causing both man and boy, father and son, blood friend to blood friend, to shield their eyes. The shimmering reflections danced with rafts and rafts from the trees above. Missy slowed to a slightly perceptible turn of the wheels. It was absorbed into this momentary shining, enveloped into a universal communion.

"When one is steadfast, and one comes and goes, within that light beheld I other lamps," intoned Mr. Jesup.

"Jeremiah! Jeremiah! Is that you?!" shouted a voice from a face looking through the screened front porch.

"Ah, more beauteous my lady grows!" shouted Mr. Jesup.

He laid on the horn. It blew for several seconds. The mule's ears pricked up. The large, black mutt bounded from the porch wagging his tail. And the last of the misty dew ascended into the air, waving the colorful bow midway up through the palm trees, reminding everyone never to drown such scenes into oblivion.

Mr. Jesup jumped out of Missy.

"My lady!" he shouted, waving his hat in the air.

On the porch with the screen door open, John saw a lady with a long, flowing beige blouse and skirt, wearing boots. Holding a wide-brim bouncy hat, she smiled with a vitality and a youthfulness that belied her many years. Her chestnut hair was only slightly grayed along the sides of her face. She was tall but possessed no domineering air. She stood straight. She wore little makeup and no jewelry, except a small ruby ring. Her gray eyes were piercing in effect even from a distance.

"Look what the winds blew into the dew-dropping South! Welcome, Jeremiah Jesup—my Telemachus—from this place ye left and returned ye have in days heralding the autumnal equinox, which is to come of our land, and do I dare say our lives?" she shouted laughing with a guttural sound that came from deep within.

"Let the years roll on!" shouted Mr. Jesup.

"Oh…I wonder," she responded, walking down the few front porch steps toward Missy.

They embraced, laughing. She slapped his shoulders several times.

"Do I find Penelope weaving or unweaving her rug?" Mr. Jesup asked.

"Penelope? You cunning flatterer, I do wish. The Athenian threads I weave are from a more transcendent loom. I faithfully expected your entrance with hope. What in the world…" she started and then paused when her gray eyes espied John. "Well, Jeremiah, what do we have here? You been sowing?"

Mr. Jesup explained to her the mission of his journey with John and the need to call John's mother.

"Come here, John," said Mr. Jesup.

John climbed out of Missy. He walked around to meet Miss Jessie. The mules raised their heads farther up into the air. The big black mutt trotted toward Missy.

John looked at Miss Jessie, examining her full face. The gray eyes wooed him to heights so quickly that he was not aware of the ascent made. Her skin defied a single description of one shade. It was not quite light, not quite dark. As the sun dappled through the thick vegetation surrounding the house, various shading was cast along the spectrum of polarities across her face. Her chestnut hair would have been associated with many nations and tribes. Her smile was universal. He was infatuated, yet this word had not yet made it into his vocabulary. In fact, he could not articulate what he was feeling. John smiled. He wanted her to call him Johnnie.

She then proclaimed, pointing to John, "This traveler brought along by you, Jeremiah, was well shepherded no doubt. You, Jeremiah, are his heaven warring champion, his Michael, journeying with him over the vast, abrupt beyond, from the tranquil to the travail of blossomed flesh. Welcome, welcome, welcome; come in and let me prepare scrambled eggs, sausage, and grits for my hungry Aeneas and Ascanius. Life in the spirit is only half a life, and a hearty breakfast feeds the soul any time of the day."

The trio walked into the cracker shack.

"You know where the phone is, Jeremiah. Speak in code, if need be, or speak as if the world is listening. There are a set of new ears in the area that can't seem to get enough satisfaction knowing other people's business. Always lusting for bits and pieces of this and that, that and this. You'll hear the breathing. At times, it truly is a party."

As they walked through the large front room that ran the length of the house, John noticed an upright piano against one wall. Above the keyboard a paper scroll was attached. He wondered what it was. The furniture was very spartan. Yet there was a beauty and symmetry in its simplicity. Lightweight rugs of various shades of brown were strewn haphazardly across the wooden floor. Pictures that reflected scenes from the surrounding area adorned the walls. Palm trees of various descriptions and interpretations were the predominant subject of the canvases. Next to the door in the kitchen, the head of a twelve-point buck hung. His expression was of a bemused bewilderment before the fatal shot froze it in place. This startled John while entering the kitchen with its wide, long table and black stove. Wood was stacked in one corner of the room. He wondered how long the buck had been hanging on the wall. His thoughts circled back to the connecting room.

"Have a seat," said Miss Jessie. "But first, over in the corner at the end of the shelf, hand me that bowl of eggs."

"Yes, ma'am," said John.

"You can call me Miss Jessie."

"Yes ma'am."

"I'll get the sausage hanging in the smoking house. Just stuffed the innards last week. Fresh and spicy it ought to be."

She left the kitchen and went outside. Mr. Jesup and John walked around the room, noticing various jars of all shapes and sizes containing fig preserves and other jams. Apples, corn, tomatoes, and oranges were neatly stacked on the shelves.

Walking back into the kitchen, Miss Jessie managed to grab several pieces of wood for the stove. She lifted one of the cast iron covers on top of the stove. There was a cast iron handle made to fit the groove in the lid to accomplish the task. She threw the pieces of wood into the circular hole. After stuffing discarded newspapers on top of the wood, she threw a lighted match into the mix. Flames leapt into the air.

"Everyone have a seat, and we will talk while I cook," she said.

While cracking the eggs open two at a time with one hand, she said, "'John,' was this your father's name?"

"Yes…Miss Jessie."

"Are you named after your father?"

"Yes."

"So you're a junior."

"I am a third."

"Oh dear…Will there be a fourth?"

"What do you mean?"

"Never mind; you will understand soon enough. Let Jeremiah tell you. But my guess is there won't be, so don't worry about it. Look in that ice box over yonder and hand me some butter. It's over the ice."

But John did worry about it. Some time passed before he understood the implications of those comments.

John walked over to the dark brown chest with three doors. One door ran the whole length of the ice box on the right side. The other two were of different shapes on the left. There were three handles. He hesitated.

"Top left!" she shouted.

He opened the door with a little difficulty. After a quick tug upward, he managed to open it. The coolness of the air flowed over his face. He wanted to stand there for a few minutes.

"Thank you, the third. Do you like your name?"

"I guess."

"It's the one given to you. If you don't like it, then write a book and create your own favorite name."

Mr. Jesup came back into the room. "John, your mother wasn't at home, so we will try again later."

"Yes, sir."

"Hand me the salt and pepper, John."

"I didn't hear any breathing, Jessie. So I guess we are still strangers in this area."

Miss Jessie laughed. The sausage started spitting in the grease. The over easy eggs were bubbling around their circular sides.

"Did you want to come to this exotic land, John?" she asked.

John stopped to think.

"I think I did. It's different. Mr. Jesup says that we are on an adventure."

"I hope you take it like I have. For me, nothing lovelier or healthier could have been found. But like everything, everyone, and everyplace, it has got its bad and good sides and days."

The aroma of the sausage was permeating the air of the kitchen.

"What do you like to do?"

"I play the piano."

"You like it?"

"Yes, ma'am."

"'Yes, Miss Jessie.'"

"Miss Jessie."

"Get teased about it?"

John was silent.

"Just as I thought." She began salting the eggs.

"It hurts, doesn't it?"

John remained quiet. He felt ashamed. He didn't want to talk about it. She flipped the sausage over.

"Remember you're not alone, son. You're not alone. Is he, Jeremiah?"

"You got that right," responded Mr. Jesup. "I am going to try the call again. Be right back."

Mr. Jesup left the kitchen.

"I've been teased and taunted all my life. I've been slapped and hit and called a no-good whore." John wasn't quite sure what that last word meant, but he knew it wasn't a compliment.

"Hand me the bread over yonder and that block of cheese."

John did so.

"And another thing: don't try to make people like you. I tried that. God knows I tried that. I ended up being all things to all people, and it was killing me, killing me. Even married a man I secretly despised because I wanted people to like me, think I was normal, whatever that means. Thank God he was a bloodsucker who found out that here in this wilderness, he was up against something much bigger than a bloodsucker like him. So he flew the coop."

She threw a dish rag into the sink and laughed.

"No sir, you end up doing no one any good, including yourself. And eventually, it may take time, but bloodsuckers end up sucking blood out of themselves!"

That was another term John was going to ask Mr. Jesup about later.

She looked at John and pointed the stirring fork with grease drippings at him and muttered in a low tone, "There is a place inside each person, a place where time slides by and you don't even realize it. No, sir, it may take time to understand that place. And for you, that place is John the Third. Treat it like royalty. When you find bits and pieces of it, just hang on and feed it. If someone puts you down or slaps you around, metaphorically speaking, you hold your head high with dignity and ignore it. Shrug it off."

Tears welled in her eyes.

"Ever had any whiskey?"

"I don't think so."

"Ever had a real bad cold?"

"A few."

"Then I bet you've had some or something nearly like it. Hand me that fancy red glass bottle over next to the ice box. I'm going to spice up our eggs. Sprinkle a little fire water over them."

John walked over toward the bottle. He picked it up gingerly, not wanting to drop it and spoil the contents. It had a pungent odor lurking around the edges. He carefully set it down next to the eggs.

"Yes sir, do good and be true when you can. I didn't find that place until I came here. This place gave me oxygen and blood to live off of. Solitude is sometimes the best society. Sometimes. But even here, it can get rough. It has slapped me; slapped me silly at times. But I knew this is where I needed to be. I would just pick myself back up, turn the other cheek, and go back at it. Something primal about this wilderness that sprouts oranges, and flowers, and—ha ha—fountains of youth. Something that goes right to the earth itself. Which reminds me, there is something I want to give you. But it can wait until tomorrow morning."

She looked out the kitchen window.

"And you know, one of the good things about this place is that it was here, right here, I met Jeremiah Jesup. I can see him walking up that dirt driveway now carrying on with his yelling and shouting!"

"John, come here, your mother wants to speak to you!" shouted Mr. Jesup from the next room.

The Morning After

Petite Orange Tree

"Now on to what I have to give you!" shouted Miss Jessie as the trio exited the cracker shack through the screened back door located in the larder room the next morning. There was a porch to cross, which was an extension of the porch from the front of the house. The big black mutt was lounging on the back steps sunning. He jumped to all fours when Miss Jessie threw open the screened back door. She adjusted her hat, which had a tendency to slip from her head, while talking at the same time.

"I have a greenhouse. Not much in size really, but it's enough for me to work in and keep busy."

She led the group with Mr. Jesup to one side. John walked behind the two, trying not to lag far behind. The big black mutt decided to trot next to John. John wanted to pet the dog but was not sure of the reaction. A run-in with a beautiful rooster at the age of five, fueled by a desire to stroke the pretty feathers, ended with the bird on John's shoulders pecking the top of his head. A battle scar on John's left shoulder remained in plain view to this day. The rooster was dinner's main course the next Sunday.

Walking through the orange groves, John saw the shady woods and sunny plains. Birds on the branches of tree were warbling, heralding their entrance into the environs. On one faraway limb, an owl was perched. The sun enlightened the earth, massaging the ground, making its breathing deeper and livelier. A world where God's smile was unforeseen. The trio began walking faster. They turned a corner of tall cedars clustered on both sides of the pathway surrounded by flowery herbs. As if arising from the living soil, a glass shed with a red brick base appeared. The glass roof angled into three gables across the length of the building. Vines covered most of the exterior, tangled, thick, and meshed into Gordian knots running in all directions. John was wondering how they would enter. He noticed a small glass door as they approached, cleared of any verdant growth. The door was slightly ajar. Miss Jessie opened it with several forward thrusts. She looked back at John and said, "Enter, Telemachus!"

Mr. Jesup and John followed, while the big black mutt heard a noise off in the distance and decided to discover the unseen.

"Let's see. I put it right over in this back corner where there is constant sun through the day."

Stacks of papers of all shapes and sizes were piled about randomly as if in a forest of oaks, where the transformation of the wood was meshed and molded into thin sheets for writing upon.

"Citrus sinensis! The modified berry that has proven the boon and balm of my existence in these tropical environs! Come, John, closer in!"

Miss Jessie stepped forward to put her arm around John's shoulder, leading him toward her gift. John saw a small tree, shrub-like, about the same height as he, in a large tin pail. The green leaves were basking in the rays of the sun.

"What is it?" asked John.

"It is the makings of an orange tree—the navel variety—a sweetness and charm that can turn the toxic into a tonic of good will—sourness is a stranger and seldom visits. It's like certain people you want to be around."

She winked at John.

"Where are the oranges?"

"They're coming; their seeds are gestating into a future hesperidium of wonder and delight!"

John walked to the plant and began stroking the leaves carefully so as not to damage the verdant foliage.

"You and Jeremiah have a new traveling companion. When you settle down to wherever it is you land, he will help you plant it in wherever it is that best suits a productive growth. I believe you and this plant will about the same time come into the fruition of what you were created to be. No shade, no hiding for this plant or you, but out in full view, celebrating."

"Well, John, what do you tell Miss Jessie?" asked Mr. Jesup.

"Thank you. We will take care of this tree. I want to see it grow. I want to see the oranges one day."

Miss Jessie hugged John.

"The place of refueling has not changed. Tell Carl hello for me," instructed Miss Jessie.

Mr. Jesup stood silently looking into her gray eyes.

"Wanderlust all my days," he whispered.

"I don't know about that. Perhaps the treasure is in your own backyard?"

"Perhaps…come on, John. We've got two more stops, then on to your aunt's house before your mother has a heart attack."

John extended his hand to Miss Jessie. He bowed. She did as well and then tousled his hair.

"Thank you again for your gift," John said.

"Remember—area with full sun, avoid closets, and follow a well-watered schedule."

Mr. Jesup and John walked from the front portals of the cracker shack to Missy. The satisfied big black mutt followed John, smacking his lips. Mr. Jesup checked the tires.

Missy sputtered and came to life. As she pulled away, Miss Jessie stood waving, adjusting her hat. After Missy turned the next corner and disappeared among the palm trees, Miss Jessie winced.

She cursed and muttered, "Where's that bottle?"

Rice Cemetery

Momento Mori

"You've discovered one of my great secrets," said Mr. Jesup.

"What's that?" asked John.

"How I got my green thumb."

"How?"

"From Miss Jessie. She taught me all I needed to know to get started."

"I like Miss Jessie."

"I felt you would. What I owe her is beyond anything I could ever do or say."

"I think it would be fun to live with her."

"Hmm…I don't know, John. I don't know. Perhaps. Visiting and living with someone are two different things. She is a bright, living thing full of life and energy. I think it pays not to fly too close to the sun if you can't take the heat. And that goes whether you are a man or a woman."

At the time, John pretended like he understood and said, "Oh, I see."

John turned to look at the orange tree situated on the back floorboard. The leaves were fluttering in the breeze, waving at all that passed.

"One more stop in this area, John. Then on to the heartland."

As the secondary highway wove its way over hilly flatlands, lakes appeared with greater frequency. Swamplands were interspersed with timberlands.

"Look, Mr. Jesup!" shouted John.

There appeared an expansive field where cowboys were galloping around in circles heading steer off in the distance.

"I bet you never thought you would see something like that down here."

"I thought cowboys were only out west."

"There are cowboys everywhere, everywhere, even if a person doesn't realize it. We call them cowboys 'crackers.'"

Mr. Jesup slowed Missy so they could enjoy the scene. But soon the road wound around a bend and forced them to move on.

Several miles down farther, Mr. Jesup turned off the secondary highway onto a dirt gravel road. A sense of dread came over John. It reminded him of that other dirt gravel road, and he wondered where this one would lead. Mr. Jesup was very still. John looked at him and saw a singular, deadening seriousness he had not seen before.

On both sides of the road were tall trees, but many were without branches. Their trunks were gray, rotten on the inside. No birds were seen swooping among the limbs. Periodically, a patch of trees appeared, looking like spent matchsticks after lighting a fire. They were standing straight or slightly tilting, charred in midair.

The dirt gravel road circled around on itself. Bigger pieces of rock were strewn about, some on the road. Missy had to swerve to miss running over the debris. On the other end of the circle was another road that turned in a different direction. Desiccated woods were the portals to a field of stubble and muck. They drove for several minutes then stopped.

"Come on, John. We won't be long. We are paying our respects."

They got out of Missy. Mr. Jesup waited until John walked over to him.

"Remember, John, I am right here. I have been here many times before."

He took John's hand. They walked out into a messy, murky field. John thought he saw on top of a tree nearby a ghastly buzzard. A cool, slight breeze blew. Their feet were being weighed down by the slush. But on they walked. A clearing unfolded that contained no stunted, maligned growth at all. Crabgrass carpeted the area, giving it a sense of serenity. They entered. Mr. Jesup slowed his pace. John watched his steps. When they reached what appeared to be the center of the area, they stopped.

"Look around you, John," whispered Mr. Jesup.

He did. He noticed uneven, broken slabs of granite sticking out of the ground. Several slabs were larger than the others. Some slabs were grouped together. In some places, there were no slabs at all. There was a still silence.

"This represents part of my past," muttered Mr. Jesup.

John looked up at Mr. Jesup, who was looking, in turn, up into the blue sky.

"No, I cannot pull in the leviathan with a fishhook!" Mr. Jesup shouted.

Mr. Jesup then bowed his head. He stood still for several minutes. John noticed birds flying around in the distance. Birds of strange shape and form. Birds he had never seen before. Birds whose calls were of sadness and lament. Cries not to be comforted.

"Patience! Patience! Hope in patience!" Mr. Jesup's voice echoed out among the fields. John recalled the other Patience. He wondered of that animal. He wondered of Tom and Long John. He expected them to ride in from the horizon at any moment.

"This is our future, John, a memento mori, memento mori."

John did not understand, but he felt an uncanny quietness in himself. He saw a snake slithering from the grass into the rocky soil.

"This is where we are all heading."

John became scared.

"But have no fear, John, no fear. This is only a doorway into a better world."

John wanted to go back to Missy.

"Yes sir, yes sir. No telling how many people were put out here. They were my people, for the most part. I know other Johns are out here, though. You see, these people had names like you and me, even if it was only one name or some nickname describing them."

John looked around. He became less afraid.

"No one here had enough money to etch their names deeply in stone. But some tried, some tried. But the wind and rain just wiped it out in time anyways. If you look closely, you might glimpse an occasional letter of an eighteen or nineteen something. But that's it. They weren't able to dig deep enough."

Mr. Jesup took John's hand.

"I don't know their names. But I feel their spirit just the same. They are not dead, no sir, they are not dead. They are speaking to us now. Even with nothing carved on these stones, they still speak. My people are here, maybe some of yours as well."

"Let's go back to Missy; she may be getting lonely."

As they walked, Mr. Jesup continued talking and looking around the area. "This is where I started to breathe, John. This is where I was passed around. Way before Zion. I was passed around by people who were in turn passed around. I don't know where Jeremiah Jesup, the name, came from. Somebody somewhere started calling me that, and it stuck. I would like to think I was named after the prophet. Then one day I went to Miss Jessie's home because she needed help harvesting her oranges for the market. So that's when we got to know each other and where my book learning on how to grow plants and flowers began as well. She wanted to call me Homer. But I said no, Jeremiah was fine by me."

John remained silent.

"Then one glorious Sunday, I came to know the Lord after a revival meeting. It was not far from here, so that afternoon I walked out here to be by myself. I was walking around. I kicked the foundations of this earth, not knowing what was going to happen next to me. And then my eye caught the glimmer of a stone, a red stone not like any I had seen before. I picked it up."

Mr. Jesup reached into his pocket and showed John the stone.

"I think it's a ruby. Not sure, though. I don't really want to find out—don't think it's important to find out. What's important is how I found it. It came out of the same ground that my people had traveled through. It was like an 'amen' to me as a child of God. And 'amen' to my name. It was a blessing. I began to live that day in a new way. I had received unexpectedly I could overcome with God no matter the bumps in the road ahead."

John looked at the red stone.

"It shines," John said.

"Yes, it does at that. And when your mother asked me to bring you down here to Florida land, I knew I was meant to, because of something else that had come out of nowhere."

"What was that?" asked John.

Mr. Jesup reached back into his pocket. He pulled out a dirty brown coin.

"Your father gave me this the last time he was home. It was like a commission to me. It was like he trusted me to look after things for him. To take his place, if need be. And in a way, I wondered if he knew something deep down inside himself."

"He gave me one, too, Mr. Jesup," said John.

"He did?!"

"Yes, sir, it's in my pocket."

John reached into his pocket and showed Mr. Jesup.

"You see, son, he trusted you to look after things as well!"

"I guess so."

They arrived at Missy. John looked back over the nameless clearing. He wondered if it was just possible that his father, too, was lying unmarked in a similar place in another part of the world.

Mirk-wood

*Mystery is a shadow, a dream, branches
pointing towards the heavens.*

"Why don't you curl up in the back seat and get some rest, John? We've got one more stop and then it's to your aunt's house."

"I'm not sleepy."

"Let's try it out anyway. Your head will be nodding before you know it. You're in safe hands."

Mr. Jesup opened the back gate of Missy and retrieved a blanket and pillow.

"Here. This pillow is special. Carries a lot of dreams. You may even see angels climbing up and down stairs from heaven."

John thought of the moon and the arm he saw embracing it many moons ago.

John crawled into the back seat. He arranged the blanket and pillow, wondering what angels looked like.

The engine sputtered to running with a slight hesitancy. Missy bounced about a bit in the field with a certain steadiness of tempo. John heard the tires meeting the asphalt pavement of the secondary road.

John stared at the roof of the car wondering how any angel could get through that solid surface.

Then John looked out the top of the windows and saw the tops of tall water cypresses swish past, with the morning in russet mantle climbing the ladder to high noon. What particularly caught his attention were large, elongated branches jutting out both sides of the tree trunks with rutted arms and finger-like extensions resembling outstretched claws. Some seemed to be alive, pulsating back and forth, swaying in one direction then another, up and then down into the sky. The tops of the water cypresses seemed to move closer and closer to the window, the Spanish mosses filling out any spaces, with their extensions flowing out into the air as the trains of long evening dresses, dancing across a room.

They seeped into the back seat through the crack of the window until they eventually filled the entire space and covered John from head to toe. He felt a warm sensation, an embrace, with the claws massaging his upper torso and shoulders, finding those tiny muscles in him sensitive to the warm movement of its fingers. He wanted to return the embrace, to wrestle with it, but could not. Try as he might, he could not. He could only lie still as the caressing continued. Then suddenly, he felt uplifted into the air. Higher and higher he was carried. Peering through the claws, he saw fields and fields of planets stretching into the celestial darkness. The arms of the claws embraced him into their folds—tighter and tighter.

Then he was turned, looking toward the earth. It stretched endlessly in every compass direction. He felt he could not be seen. From this vantage point, he could watch anyone, and they not know it. He could speed through the air, dipping down among cedar branches, saving people from death and destruction and they do not know it. Imagining their conversations revealing inner thoughts and motivations. Imagining their lives, the plots, the dramas and designing the events, weaving climaxes and meanings with great dexterity and intricate complications. His attire spoke of humane masculinity. He would exhibit no anima for fear of taunts and threats. He would strike, strike those ivory keys. The enfolding arms rocked him back and forth. He felt a warmth. He wanted to soar higher and higher and farther and farther. But the claw was grasping around his wrist tighter and tighter. Branches violently withdrew. The Spanish moss disintegrated into a thousand slithers of dark hairs. A bright light shone on his face. He saw the tops of sullen water cypress trees. John could see they no longer swished by in his view.

"John!" shouted Mr. Jesup.

John started.

"Hey, son, wake up."

John looked around.

"Are we home?"

"Almost. 'Not sleepy,' he says. Hmm. It didn't take much for you to check out the last hundred miles," laughed Mr. Jesup.

"Where are we?"

"Just one more stop to visit before we reach your aunt's house, I promise," said Mr. Jesup.

The Singing Tower

A Tall Mound of Earth
Lincoln
Get Away

Missy weaved her way through hilly terrain spotted with cattle and large oaks. Gradually, the land flattened into marshy, wooded plots before once again gently rising and falling into slight foothills on a ribbon-like road that meandered suddenly into groves of hefty green trees, loaded with oranges.

"Look! Mr. Jesup!" yelled John.

"I see! I see John. The heart of Florida land—the orange groves. The heart beats right here."

"Do you think my tree will ever get that big?"

"It could. It could. Just have to wait and see how all the elements of this world come together to allow such," responded Mr. Jesup.

"Orange…"

"Yes, that sweet edible berry with sweet edible pulp on their insides. The color of the rind gives it its name. They are called what they are. They like it, too."

Off in the distance, John saw a tall tower rising toward the clouds.

"What's that?" John asked.

"Citrus Tower, but we don't have time to stop there. No sir, we're staying right here on 17 and heading toward a tower that sings."

"It sings?" asked John.

"At certain times of the day it does. It takes you places, John. Yes, sir, it takes you places."

John could only imagine moving lips with jaws going up and down and an Adam's apple bobbing on certain notes.

"I have to see that," said John.

"You will. I first saw it a long time ago right after it was first built. It's never left me since. It's never left me alone. At times, it pulls on me like a thread. I could go to the ends of the earth and it could still pull me back, even at the oddest of times. Yes, sir, I hope you see what I have seen. Hear what I have heard."

The orange groves continued expanding farther and farther into the horizon with an occasional intermission of a small town where Missy was forced to travel through rows of buildings and over the occasional railroad track at 35 mph.

The land flattened once more. There appeared rising over the immediate horizon a cluster of oak and orange trees on a very tall mound of earth. An ornate, pink-gray tower rose expansively into the skies, growing taller as Missy approached. Its cathedral-looking façade lent an air of solemnity and calm around it. Its gothic diadem with seven pelican spires of pink and gray marble majestically stood, brushing the lower reaches of the heavens. Multi-colored tiled windows adorned the entire circumference of the tower below its crown, as the tower slightly expanded its width as the side resolutely cascaded into the arrangement of green trees gathered around its base.

Mr. Jesup rolled down his window. John followed suit. Faintly through the air, sounds of lilting melody whispered in and through the breezes flowing into Missy.

"Oh, Ariel, my brave spirit, how thee sing!" exclaimed Mr. Jesup.

"What are they playing? I can't make it out," said John.

"Mysterium tremendum, mysterium tremendum," the gleaming Mr. Jesup whispered.

"Oh," responded John as though he understood.

Mr. Jesup began whistling as they rounded a bend approaching a small town. John no longer could see the singing tower easily because they had passed it and were heading farther south. John thought perhaps the entrance lay through the row of buildings down the road in front of them. But Mr. Jesup slowly applied the brakes. He turned left off of Highway 17. Up a steep hill they rode. They reached its crest and descended. An entrance sign appeared. And then as though it were stepping out of another room in a house, the singing tower sauntered into view.

Mr. Jesup turned to the left again. The entrance gate was in front of them. Mr. Jesup pulled over to the side of the road.

"Open the glove compartment, John," he said.

"Yes, sir."

"See a long, beige envelope?"

"Yes, sir." He recognized it as the one his mother had given to Mr. Jesup.

"Hand it here, please, sir."

"Yes, sir."

Mr. Jesup took the envelope and laid it on the seat beside him.

"Come on. Let's ride right straight into the gale wind of the mountain lake sanctuary. The direct approach, I say."

John looked at Mr. Jesup. He was mouthing words with no voice. John followed suit but in his own way was thinking about their travels thus far.

Missy made a steady, smooth approach. She stopped the entrance gate. An elderly man wearing thick-lens glasses stepped out.

"Good afternoon!" he said.

"Good afternoon, sir," said Mr. Jesup. "Come to walk around and see the tower."

"Beautiful day for it. Not too hot, not too much humidity."

"Yes, sir."

The elderly man looked into the car and saw John. John smiled and made a slight wave of his hand.

"Been here before?"

"I have. But this is John's first trip. We're on the way to his aunt's house."

John smiled again.

"I see. You like music, son?" asked the entrance guard.

"Yes, sir. I play the piano."

"And I am a gardener by trade. This place served as an inspiration to me in days gone by," said Mr. Jesup.

"Well then, both of you are in the right place. Let's see—one adult, one child—that will be five dollars."

"One Lincoln face. How appropriate," Mr. Jesup remarked.

"That's right. Only one is needed to get you in," the elderly man responded smiling.

Mr. Jesup handed over the Lincoln bill.

"Thank you much. Straight ahead as you know. Both of you have a good time."

"We will," said Mr. Jessup.

Missy pulled away. John once more waved at the guard, who returned the gesture.

"Here, John, you can put this back." Mr. Jesup handed John the long, beige envelope.

John did as instructed and slammed the glove box door shut.

"Those are pearls that were his eyes: nothing of him that doth fade, but doth suffer a sea-change into something rich and strange," intoned Mr. Jesup.

Missy meandered through the orange groves. A sudden hard left turn cast the singing tower into immediate view. There it stood—jutting out from among the bushy orange groves, an epithalamion ready to shoot forth life from its firm, pulsating pink and gray marbled edifice, leaf-whelmed with the hood of many a bushy-bowered wood.

As they twisted and turned, John thought of the old cedar bush at his first home. Now and in this space he was riding that used popsicle stick named Missy. Together they were traveling among the verdant branches loaded with newborn oranges of various sizes, rather than the limpid pods of cedar bush seeds. After several more turns—and some near misses of overlying branches—they safely landed in an asphalt parking lot below the left side of the singing tower. John quickly looked around outside his window. He saw no killer wasps buzzing about.

"Come on, John, let's go explore."

John jumped out of the car. He felt the warmth of Missy's hood as he walked around to the front of the engine. Looking toward the incline of the path leading to the gardens, Mr. Jesup stepped into view. John saw the side profile of Mr. Jesup and studied him carefully for the first time, paying attention to him, wondering the whole history of this man who had brought him to this place, trying to catch a glimpse of the ineffable with no one being the wiser. A song from the chiming carillons lilted through the air.

"Now I hear them. They are welcoming us. Come on," said Mr. Jesup again.

John felt he could satisfy his curious spirit to his heart's content without any fear of the weeping and gnashing of teeth lurking around, breathing down his neck. They walked together, with Mr. Jesup's hand on John's shoulder.

The opening portals of sabal palms, live oaks, and ferns graced the entrance with a winding path of dried leaves leading to other Edenic vistas around multiple bends. It was an asymmetry of living things that was symmetrical, offering a pleasing invitation to explore. One turn led to another farther up the path with no tether from behind that invited punishment if not adhered to. Dreams, along with the clouds, were glimmering rich possibilities as a thousand tweeting birds were twittering through the air. It seemed any winged injury would invite cure. Looking up, John could see shafts of light through the leaves. Here John feasted: lovely all is. Mr. Jesup and John followed the path around another bend. The air was engulfed by sweet smelling scents.

"Tea olive bushes," said Mr. Jesup, pointing to their left.

As the lingering mists melted into the air, into the thin air the singing tower emerged, standing massive and majestic. Crowned with its eight heron figures, the jewels encased on the windows below the apex of the tower reflected the approaching late afternoon rays from the sun. The sleek pond extending from the tower in turn reflected its entire length, as two white swans glided across the pond's surface, hiding the furious movement of their webbed feet below the waterline. The swans appeared intermittently among the many, varied-colored camellia and azalea bushes. This King tower invited kneeling of heart, soul, and mind—a distinctive altar within a world full of altars.

Mr. Jesup and John turned, facing the base of the tower, enraptured with a silent solemnity. The Florida coquina rock of the tower, checkered with light shades of flamingo and gray Georgia marble, shimmered and glowed with the warmth and light coming from the rejoicing champion running its course through the final stretches of the day. A closed-panel gold door into the singing tower flamed like a burning bush. From this ember door, a small bridge over a moat led to a closed gate that was locked. John saw this. He wished could have entered the tower and explored its interior space.

"Let's go look at the sundial," said Mr. Jesup as he led the way to another side.

John looked ahead. He saw a couple standing. It was a man and a woman. Both wore scornful frowns. The woman turned. She looked at John, and then looked at Mr. Jesup. She touched the man's arm. He turned and looked at John and Mr. Jesup, too. He wore small glasses. His eyes were small. He squinted. He was also tall and heavy-set, completely bald with the exception of thin strands of hair around the sides of his head. The couple looked at each other. He whispered in the woman's ear. They started walking toward John and Mr. Jesup on one side. Mr. Jesup, looking at the tower, muttered, "Dedicated and presented for visitation to the American people." The couple walked behind John and Mr. Jesup. As they passed, John thought he heard something menacing from the mouth of the man. It was a low, hissing sound. John was terrified. He wanted to go back to Missy. He looked at Mr. Jesup, who was moving his lips.

"It won't pay to look back," whispered Mr. Jesup to John.

Suddenly from the top of the tower, the bells began to sing. Mr. Jesup turned his head toward the heavens as the music played.

"Yes, sir, how great thou art," said Mr. Jesup.

For several minutes, they stood. The clouds from above drifted in front of the sun, causing the shadows on the sundial to fade in and out.

John looked to see if the couple was in the area, but they had disappeared.

"I've got one more thing to show you, John, before we make tracks."

They walked away from the silent tower to the opposite side of their approach. The swans had disappeared. The gardens were quieter. The hushed stillness screamed in John's ear.

"Through here," whispered Mr. Jesup.

They crouched through an opening among the camellia bushes. A small, worn path weaved its way through the gathered plants and trees. They were tied and bunched together like bushels of wheat. Mr. Jesup and John emerged onto a hill that sloped down to an open meadow. There was a driveway at the base of the hill. It led to a brown, stucco, Mediterranean mansion with a dark roof. Off to the left side of the driveway, a tiled path graced with boxwoods led to the double glass doors on one side of the house.

"I used to know someone who worked in that house. Let's go take a peek. It doesn't look like anyone is home," said Mr. Jesup.

"Are you sure it's okay?" asked John.

"It'll be all right. The person I knew may still work here. We're just paying a friendly call. Besides, from a distance, you and I look like we might belong here, if we act normal."

John was not quite sure what acting normal would look like, although he found out later in life. Without hesitation, he walked alongside Mr. Jesup as they went down the hill and onto the driveway and then followed the tiled path to the mansion. They saw an oval archway that embraced the double door in front of them.

"I want to show you something, Mr. Chopin," said Mr. Jesup.

A fountain was centered on the patio in front of the oval archway. Off to the left side was a large water oak. Palms were gracing both sides of the entrance. Mr. Jesup walked to the left of the fountain and John to the right. They met once more on the other side.

"I want to show you what's in this room," said Mr. Jesup.

They slowly walked to the glass doors.

"Be careful not to smudge the windows, John. Bessie would not like that," said Mr. Jesup.

They peered into the room. To the left side was the largest piano that John had ever seen. It seemed almost as long as the length of the room.

"Wow, it's a piano," whispered John.

"Yes sir, and it's a mighty grand, a mighty grand. Perhaps one day you will be able to play on something like that."

"I hope so."

"I bet you will. My, oh my, John, look what's sitting on top of the piano," said Mr. Jesup.

It was a large brown vase containing tall green stalks, with several large scarlet blossoms, black edges with occasional indentions and tiny yellow pods in its center.

"What is it?" asked John.

"That is what you call an amaryllis picotee."

"I've never seen anything like it before."

"Sometimes it takes a while to bloom, but with the right kind of love and attention, you can get what you see before you now. Sometimes it blossoms overnight."

"Sitting on top of a piano."

"Yes, sir, sitting on top of a piano, John. Come on, we'd better get back to Missy. The day is ending, and I need to get you to your aunt's house before dark."

They went back the same way they had come. When walking through the gathered plants and trees, Mr. Jesup suddenly stopped.

"Wait a minute, John," he whispered, peering through one of the openings.

John stopped and could not hear anything. Presently, he heard a low murmuring of voices. He looked through one of the openings. Off in the distance, John saw three people turning toward the path to the silent tower. It was the man and the woman they had seen earlier. They were accompanied by a policeman.

When they were out of view, Mr. Jesup said with a calm voice, "Okay, John, walk regular-like; don't run. Keep a steady pace with me, and whatever you do, don't look back. Come on."

He followed Mr. Jesup's instructions. And for what seemed like forever, they weaved themselves though the garden and trees and arrived back at Missy.

As Missy took them out of the parking lot, through the orange groves and entrance gate, John kept looking forward. Mr. Jesup waved at the guard.

"Well, John, we're almost there. Roll your window down. Let's get some fresh air in here."

After John did so, he looked back to see if anyone was following them. But instead, he heard from behind the tower singing once more. After a few moments, he turned back to see what was on the road ahead, thinking of the large, brown piano crowned with the blossoming amaryllis picotee.